OAK
HOLLOW

DAN MCDOWELL

Black Rose Writing | Texas

ISBN: 978-1-68433-795-8
PUBLISHED BY BLACK ROSE WRITING
www.blackrosewriting.com

Printed in the United States of America
Suggested Retail Price (SRP) $17.95

Oak Hollow is printed in EB Garamond

*As a planet-friendly publisher, Black Rose Writing does its best to eliminate unnecessary waste to reduce paper usage and energy costs, while never compromising the reading experience. As a result, the final word count vs. page count may not meet common expectations.

DEDICATION

ECCLESIASTES 12:1-8

Remember your Creator
in the days of your youth,
before the days of trouble come
and the years approach when you will say,
"I find no pleasure in them"—
before the sun and the light
and the moon and the stars grow dark,
and the clouds return after the rain;
when the keepers of the house tremble,
and the strong men stoop,
when the grinders cease because they are few,
and those looking through the windows grow dim;
when the doors to the street are closed
and the sound of grinding fades;
when people rise up at the sound of birds,
but all their songs grow faint;
when people are afraid of heights
and of dangers in the streets;
when the almond tree blossoms
and the grasshopper drags itself along
and desire no longer is stirred.
Then people go to their eternal home
and mourners go about the streets.
Remember him—before the silver cord is severed,
and the golden bowl is broken;
before the pitcher is shattered at the spring,
and the wheel broken at the well,
and the dust returns to the ground it came from,
and the spirit returns to God who gave it.
"Meaningless! Meaningless!" says the Teacher.
"Everything is meaningless!"

OAK HOLLOW

SPRING 1991

CHAPTER ONE

JAKE CALHOUN convinced himself that six-o-five held him hostage despite no evidence. Flinging his typewriter across the room, he yelled, "That's better. That... is the way this should end."

He bundled up the tweed belt in the southeast corner of the room, cinching it around his neck as he stood on the end table. As the clock flashed 2:05, a catchy *Dire Straits* number played in the background.

His weary voice creaked from the sleepless nights, "I can't do this anymore. You show me things, you tell me things. You show me things, you tell me things... and what do I end up with? Huh? A warped mind... I just can't," he said, kicking the used bottles of whiskey from the table. "No more empty promises this time, Dorse. This time... I'm done. I hope the empty desk was what you guys were after."

He kicked the table beneath before the flashing clock could reach 2:06. The paper fed through the top of the fractured unit had only three lines completed as it leaned against the indented sheetrock.

The room's novelty is something to marvel. No matter how many times I study it, new features catch my attention, from the gold-plated wall sconces and matching fixtures to the elaborate elegance of the lavatory; I'm led to question what the true incentive to restore The Oak Hollow Hotel really was...

***

VIC RAMSEY sat behind his typewriter, searching for the words. The article would never write itself, and nothing could change the truth — Calhoun was gone, and he would have to pick up the slack. Hal Dorse would be on his case if he did not make cutoff time. It was an unconventional decision to continue writing about food, but it had become his obsession.

Forty-five articles on the finest restaurants in Riverton and still not a single accolade from Dorse. He is some kind of persnickety.

The simple thought process left him overanalyzing. Victor Jolon Ramsey was burned out, scorched, and left for dead in his skeptical series of columns on culinary cuisines. He possessed a background in dining, but had no experience in the kitchen itself, leaving his articles dull and lacking substance. The words were well written, but the experience was limited. There was just an unspoken technicality he struggled to finesse. Dorse would never admit it to him, and maybe he would never have to. When the promotion and raise came around the previous year, Vic was bypassed and left flat with a contract extension – not terminated or reprimanded, just accepted as good enough.

I've got to create a better column. Something that will sell. Dorse is about to recycle me to the Riverton Anvil. And then, once they dispose of me, it's the unemployment line.

Dorse approached, resting his hand on the back of his chair. "How's it coming, Ramsey?"

He sighed. "I'm not sure. I'm feeling stuck. Writer's block."

"You're in the newspaper biz, my friend," Dorse said, donning his BOSS MAN coffee mug. "There's no such thing. I know you'll find something. Write the truth... as you see it."

"What truth is there left to tell? Nothing's going to change the fact that Calhoun is gone. That leaves us a big glaring hole in the metro section."

"Yeah," Dorse sneered, finishing his last sip of late morning coffee, "I suppose you're more disposable than he ever was. I can put you on the Crimewatch column or we can put you in miscellaneous metro to fill the void."

Vic pulled out his write up and handed it over to Dorse. "Miscellaneous metro sounds ambiguous enough for me. Diversity in my life could be good. I'm to a point where TV dinners and *Murphy Brown* are the highlight of my day. It's not a miserable existence, but it's duller than it should be for a guy my age."

"It's the nineties, man," Dorse said. "Meet some women... invite 'em over. Let gravity do the rest." He turned around, checking for listeners near the reception area. "Clean-cut guy like you probably has no debts, your parents are dead, and you've learned how to play the game of life well. Women are looking for men like that — lower commitment and less recklessness. We're tamed once we get this age. You can't put a bounty on that, can you?"

Whatever you say. Leave me be... he thought.

Ramsey stood up from his chair. "Thanks. I'm going to take a lunch. I've sliced and diced every sit-down place in this town, and I'm just about out of steam. I'm ready for something new. I was going to make a run to Old Town Riverton. It's the one area I can still show my face because I didn't tear it to shreds."

"Alright," Dorse said, "I'll give you a break. I won't make you write any hit pieces over there. Explore around. Find something else worthwhile to write about. Find your morning muse." He leaned in and whispered in Vic's ear, the stench of coffee and cigarettes on his breath lingering, "Between us, I think Calhoun had a gold mine in that old hotel restoration, all kinds of interesting stuff. It's a shame his marbles dropped out of the bag all at once."

"Cold and calloused, aren't you?"

"High-pressure job, lots of visibility, and a ton of flack if you get it wrong. Thick skin's a must in this business, Ramsey. You should know that by now," Dorse said, slapping him on the back.

CHAPTER TWO

NANCY HELBENS RICHARDS and her husband (the former "Ramblin' Ron" of WGBO) stood in the oversized entryway of the Reinhold estate, studying the elegant Victorian railings and the confederate war pieces that graced the walls. She looked at their realtor, the jovial but eccentric Johnny Lathrop. The man's bleached hair was a testament to the times, while his starched plaid shirt, Levi's, and an oversized belt buckle pointed to an unmatchable character from a postmodern Western. His voice was unmistakable, a bit nasally with a whistle that would occasionally become prominent as he pronounced his S's.

"Well, folks, that brings us to the close of our tour," he said. "What do you think? Does the Reinhold estate interest you? I have to say, it is one heck of a bargain. This much square footage at this price in this zip code is unheard of."

"I think we just have some questions on the history of the property," Ron said, running his hand down the banister of the impressive staircase. "Have there been any deaths? Murders? That kind of thing?"

"Nothing worth mentioning. The late Mrs. Reinhold had an accident in the driveway, but it was a total freak thing. The poor hag hit her head on a rock and decided it was her day to meet her maker."

"Yeah, I remember hearing about that," Ron said. "I guess it's not much to sweat over. Is it, Nancy? You're the more cerebral and feeling of the two of us."

"Hmm... I think this is way out of our budget," she said, "but dreaming big, I picture Randy having a great time here, roaming the halls and exploring around. What are they asking for it again?"

"Four hundred even. Trust me, this is a real bargain. This house was on the market, vacant at seven hundred-fifty K for two years."

Get real. We can't afford this, she thought.

"Let us sleep on it, Johnny. We'll let you know," Ron said.

As morning approached, Nancy awoke early to make a cup of coffee and a lunch for Randy before school while Ron continued to snooze. The almost seven-year-old wandered into the room wearing dinosaur pajamas, and a red-headed chili-bowl cut, all too fitting for his forty-two-inch body. He was petite but overcame the shortfall with superior intellect.

"Mom, are you making me a peanut butter and jelly sandwich again? Dad told me I could just get lunch in the cafeteria now... now... that we're rich," Randy said.

"We're not rich. Is that what your father's telling you? The seeds that oddball plants in your head sure leave me scratching mine."

The boy laughed.

"Alright, scoundrel, get on to school. Don't forget your sack lunch."

"Yes, mother." He walked toward the doorway as the bus approached.

"I'll see you later. Hey, when you get home, the garage will be organized."

"Bye, mom."

She walked toward the garage where Ron's things were strewn about the room in no particular order.

My fault, too, but that man is the king of stashing. I will not get frustrated.

Shrugging her shoulders, she began organizing some of the shelves that lined the wall for a moment, until arriving upon a box.

I haven't looked at this stuff in ages.

She rifled around it, finding a variety of personal mementos, and stumbled upon her high school yearbook.

Memory lane... what gives? A few minutes won't hurt anything.

Flicking through, she perused the index.

There it is, Helbens, Nancy, 18, 36, 54, 72.

On page eighteen, her face was scribbled over with devil horns. On the bottom, blue ink was smudged in a sloppy cursive, *Nancy, Nancy, the Townwhore eyesore.*

I hate you... she thought. *You and all your name-calling!*

***

She peered out the window, waiting for Randy to arrive home from school. The room stilled reeked of Ron's dirty laundry wedged beneath the futon, despite him not coming in for days because of the clutter. A few second-rate hair metal posters, a mounted hunting rifle, and a worn guitar hung on the wall that hadn't been plucked since *Jefferson Starship* was a thing. Her appetite for decorating the home had significantly dwindled with time, and she grew apathetic to Ron's youthful interests. She played his cassette for a few minutes, finding herself singing along. As the bus pulled up, she turned it off. Randy's glowing smile showed a familiar after-school buzz, happy and chipper. He walked in, clearly not expecting her to leap out and surprise him.

"Think you're just going to sneak on past me?" she said, coming up behind and wrapping her arms around him. "You can't even make time to give me a hug anymore? What's up with that?"

"Yeah... I was putting my backpack away."

He blew air between his lips.

"What are you doing?"

"Can you teach me how to whistle?" Randy asked.

"You funnel air through your lips. It's a finesse thing."

"A what?"

"Never mind," she said.

"Teach me. I want to do v-ness."

Nancy shook her head. "Finesse..."

"What is that?"

"It's when you get so good at something that it just happens," she said. "You know, kind of like the way I make your sandwiches so perfectly."

"Yeah. When dad makes them, the jelly just goes everywhere and drips through the bread all over the lunchroom table."

"Your father isn't cut out for that, is he? He's gifted in other ways, though..."

"Like what?" he asked.

Nancy rested her hand under her chin. "The man's a professional knob turner... a button pusher."

"Enough!" he said. "Just teach me how to whistle."

Nancy shook her head at Randy, blowing air through her lips. "It's one of those things you just have to learn. Keep blowing. Get them shaped like a narrow 'o' and push air through softly."

Randy attempted to with no luck as warm air spewed between his lips.

She walked to the fridge and popped open a Flitz for herself, handing Randy a Little Man Flitz Root Beer. She pried the caps with Ron's old Swiss army knife.

"We all know who the real kingpin of the pong is, don't we?" she said. "Let's go play a few minutes before your dad comes home."

"Don't you mean, queenpin?"

"Yeah... Queenpin. That sounds better. You're a bright child." Nancy said, laughing.

They raced up the stairs, plowing into the game room. Pictures of Nancy were strewn about with vile and vulgar names written across each in permanent marker ink. Nancy stood thunderstruck as Randy chattered toward her, his words becoming incomprehensible in the moment.

"Get out, now. I've got to figure out what's going on. Not another word." She picked up the photos, studying the handwriting closer.

It's the same handwriting as the annual. Unless 'she' was wasted when she watched Randy last night.

"Do you know what this is about?" Nancy asked, her eyes narrowing, and her teeth clenched. "You have someone teaching you new words at school?"

He studied the disheveled room a moment before looking back at Nancy. "No. I'm scared, mommy."

So am I...

"Go to your room and get your Lincoln Logs. I'll come play with you for a while before dad gets back. He had another interview this afternoon. I want to put this stuff away first, though."

Randy exited the room, walking down the pictureless hallway to his own.

She picked up the last photograph, stacking it together with the others as she flipped through them again, analyzing the handwriting and the various symbols scribbled on and across her eyes and body. Some of them were peace signs, others were birds. The ones that concerned her most were the upside-down crosses drawn on her arms.

I don't even know where to start. Friggin' cops wouldn't do jack. Gosh, I'm sounding like Ron...

CHAPTER THREE

The PRIEST walked the fifth floor of the building with care while Jerry Greenwich lingered behind. Running his hands down the walls, the wise theologian recited a prayer over The Oak Hollow Hotel in its newly restored state [Jerry having kept the sixth floor closed since Calhoun's demise].

"Bless this building and all that come into it. May its owners and guests seek your face daily, knowing you will protect them, Father. May their folly never lead them astray... Show your favor and grant opportunities for your light to shine through... Amen."

The priest nodded toward Jerry and they approached the elevator. Despite no words exchanged between the pair, their mutual respect for one another remained evident. As the elevator doors closed, Jerry spoke to the priest, "Thank you for doing this. I couldn't in good conscience move forward in taking this place over without finding some kind of favor for it."

The priest maintained a silent reverence, repeating the prayer as they walked down the corridor of the sixth floor. Instead of turning around and nodding to Jerry as he had the previous five floors, he walked toward the far end, looping the prayer and getting louder and louder as he neared the darker east side.

"The lights always have an issue on this wing," Greenwich said, scratching his head. "We've called the electricians a few times and every time they come in they can never figure out what's triggering the problem. I may just shut this level down if push comes to shove. Spend some extra time near six-o-five, would you? That's where the poor bastard hung himself. I don't feel right letting anyone back in until we cleanse it. God bless him. I never saw the last article. Business has sure been slow lately. That didn't help any."

The priest looked toward Jerry, shushing him. He continued to pray as the corridor darkened, splashing holy water on the sides of the walls.

"O my Jesus, forgive us our sins. Save us from the fires of hell. Lead all souls to heaven, especially those in most need of Thy mercy. Amen."

The lights in the eastern corridor brightened. Their reflection left the priest's eyes glowing as he looked toward Greenwich. The reticent proprietor to The Oak Hollow Hotel stepped back.

"All done," the priest said. "I must get back to lead mass."

Greenwich spoke up, raising his hands in protest, "Wait a minute... we still need to pray over the seventh and eighth floors."

The priest sighed, his eyes normalizing to a darker color. "We've prayed enough. I don't want my heart's cry to fall on deaf ears."

Greenwich studied him. "What?"

The priest grabbed at his rosary necklace, kissing it. "Father God, have mercy... Jerry, this floor can be cleansed no further. The other spirits have moved on. They've been eradicated. You'll have no more trouble."

"From who?" Greenwich asked.

The priest's eyes widened as he whispered, "Wasserman... Wilkerson... The Lord whispered to me that they're all but dust and ash. Don't worry. The place can finally breathe again."

Greenwich shook his head, fumbling around in his pockets as his keys jingled. "I'd like you to come onto the next floor, please. Let's finish this right. You're being compensated for your services, remember?"

The priest turned away, evidencing eagerness to leave. "Not necessary..." he mumbled.

They entered the elevator and moved toward the back. Greenwich pressed the seven. He studied the man of great faith, waiting for a reply.

The priest's voice grew shaky, "What are you doing? I said we're finished. Take me downstairs."

Greenwich smiled, his face unfamiliar and unnatural. "Yes, we are."

Without warning, the elevator cable snapped, plummeting into the basement level of the building. As flames engulfed the space and smoke permeated within, the priest crawled across, unsure if he could remove the shrapnel now protruding from his stomach. He crawled toward Greenwich, who remained unconscious and moved the man as close to the door as possible, all the while working to pry the entry loose. His breath was sharp and short as the elevator burned.

He prayed.

"PATER NOSTER, qui es in caelis, sanctificetur nomen tuum..." The elevator door was forced open from the outside as he passed out.

***

THE PRIEST awoke as a wrinkled woman hovered above. She wrung out a wet rag as trickling droplets rolled down his forehead into the creases of his eyes. The crackle of a neighboring fire popped as the woman warmed a can of tomato soup. Looking toward it, dancing flames left him squinting. The bizarre "bag" stood in front of it, chanting to the sky in an incomprehensible tongue. Her silhouetted body stood well kept, despite a peculiar choice of abode. Slipping out of the unshapely gray smock, she donned a pin-striped pantsuit accompanied by an oxford shirt that accentuated her effeminate figure. The shimmer of the diamond necklace that dangled from her neck paired well with the leather watch and her matching moccasins.

He peered around as his eyes adapted. As droplets converged, the harsh brightness of the fire and the struggle to keep his eyes open minimized, allowing him to take in more of the extensive space. A flesh toned canvas stood on an easel next to the fire. Speaking no words to the priest, she instead opted to collect a variety of brushes from around the corner. Carrying over an exacto knife toward him, she carved into his arm, taking a small chunk.

His mind raced, but he remained unable to speak or move anything below his neck to protest.

What's happened to me? Who are you?

The woman dropped the flesh into the soup can. She looked over at him, humming a familiar tune, and dipping her fine tipped brush into the can — gradually becoming words in sing-song, "Red and yellow, black and white, they are precious in His sight."

She stroked the front of the canvas with the brush.

"You see the clash there?" she asked. "They should match up, but they don't. It's a nice contrast. You see?"

Struggling to find words, his silence spoke louder.

"I've been painting a long time," she said, looking toward him. "There are a few tricks that set apart the O'Keefe's and the Rockwell's from the rest, though. It's not technique. It's the base coat... Don't tell. These are trade secrets."

She came toward the priest, moving behind him to study the painting from a distance.

"Screw the traditionalists," she said, leaning over the fire a moment. "I make my own way and it's selling well."

She stroked the brush up and down the sides of the painting. Walking toward the fire, she pulled out another brush, allowing it to light briefly before blowing it out as its ember tip glowed. The canvas transformed as she painted in a circular motion, and a dark shape formed in the center.

"I layer all my canvases just the same before I start my paintings. Forget the primary colors. Work with what's in our bodies to influence your paint. You heat it up, mix up a base, and then you can bless the canvas with a *piece* of someone."

She went around the corner, her footsteps clanking up a ladder.

Where are you going? You've got me wondering now, he thought.

A few minutes later she returned. A man writhed aloud just above.

She grinned. "He got what he deserved... Just an intruder. There we go... native sun-baked skin. Now, that's special! No two of us are just alike, are we? Some are rosy red... others burnt brown... and then there are some that are nothing more than weathered leather bags. I can sell it all, though."

She came toward the priest and sat him up, propping him against the wall. "How many bodies go to waste in the ground? There's too much crime in the present to be concerned about who's digging around in the past."

She hoisted the shovel into the air, thrusting it into the priest with an inhuman forcefulness, his blood spilling onto the floor. She rounded the corner, picking up a pewter cup and allowing it to fill up with blood as she poured it into the soup can.

"Ah, yes. Crimson red. So beautiful... Thanks, father. Now, Jerry and I both got what we wanted out of you. Good riddance. We don't need any more men of the cloth around. Just a bunch of hot air and misguided principles. The tables are reset, and I've got plenty of room in here. Don't I?"

CHAPTER FOUR

Dinner was quiet and nothing remarkable. There was a lull in the conversation between NANCY HELBENS RICHARDS and Ron as she studied the hustle and bustle of the wait staff across the Bridgewater Restaurant.

"And that's the real reason Dukakis never became president..." he said. "It's all a big government cover-up..."

I don't think I can do this much longer. You're driving me nuts, she thought, as Ron continued to ramble.

"Islands in the Stream" by *Dolly Parton* and *Kenny Rogers* came on in the background.

"It's our song," she interrupted. "Can you shut up a minute?"

Ron tapped his finger on the table to the beat of the song, his fidgeting, further evidence to his frustration being stopped in the middle of a thought.

"Such a perfect blend of voices. Why do you keep going on about that election? It's been a couple of years now... besides, it was a landslide!" she said.

"Think what you want. I know the truth! You think he'll run again one of these days?" Ron asked, chewing on his dinner roll.

Nancy shook her head. "We'll see what happens. My interview at the hotel was smooth. I'll begin on the 30th. What are we going to do with the kid? School's out next week and you might actually find a job yourself if you can use that gift of gab of yours correctly for a change. No friggin' politics, religion, or government conspiracies, Ron!"

His eyes were drawn to the television behind Nancy's head. "Some pundits are saying the election map is going to totally reset in '92," he said, sipping on his Flitz. "I don't think we'll be that red again for a while..."

Why should I care?

She interrupted him. "I gave mom a break from watching Randy. I'm concerned with what she does when we're not around..."

Ron's eyes had gravitated to the television in the bar area.

Seriously?

"So, what do you think the little punk's worth? Twenty bucks or thirty?"

He looked over at Nancy, tucking his head back for a second and furrowing his brow. "Since when do you talk that way about the kid?"

Her eyes squinted, her voice growing tenser to match Ron's, "What way? That he's a little punk?"

Ron scoffed, shaking his head. "Exactly."

Nancy sipped her iced tea. "Remind me why I should follow your lead again? We've been an item for a while now. What do you have to show for it? Four dead-end jobs and a cumulative salary of $38,000 — your highlight, three months on the overnight shift at the Gas 'n Sip. I know you wanted out of the radio business to get your head straight, but I'm sure you were compensated better in those days. It's time to face the music. You've officially become a deadbeat dad."

Ron scrunched his nose. "Well then, why bother with me?"

She flashed a plastic grin. "You're you. And I still like you, despite all your... idiosyncrasies."

Straightening his fork and spoon back across the top of the napkin, he sighed. "What idiosyncrasies? I can't know them until you speak them."

Nancy's face reddened. "And that, Ron, is why we're on the brink of a divorce. You don't have a clue or seem to care anymore. The royal purple sheets. The plaid printed chairs. The puke green Daihatsu that you're afraid to drive. The thrift store smoking jackets. I could go on..."

"Alright, fine. You made your point. Now, let's get home to those royal purple sheets, and I'll show you what a deadbeat dad's actually worth."

"Really? It's about time. Tonight...?" she said, grinning.

"Any night you want, momma bear."

***

Ron and Nancy pulled into the driveway of their North Riverton home — a humble start that needed serious pruning and repair to be attractive for the late blooming family.

"Do you think Randy's in bed yet?" Nancy asked, unbuckling her seatbelt.

Ron turned the radio down. "What gives? You said the little guy was jumping from the coffee table to the couch before we left. Does the babysitter have the willpower to manage that?"

Nancy chuckled. "You saw her, right? Of course she does. You think I picked an attractive foreigner for the heck of it? I paid extra for that."

Ron laughed. "Brains before beauty except when babysitting boys. Ha-ha."

"You may be onto something." She smiled, tucking her arm under Ron's as they approached the house. "Happy fifth, honey."

He's such a sucker for sappy, she thought. *Be nice.*

Ron kissed her. "Happy fifth."

Nancy's jovial way lasted only a moment before she sighed.

"What's wrong?" he asked.

"It's that house we looked at, Ron. I know we can't afford it. You know it, too, but taking me there to let me roam around it was a nice, cheap way to thrill this uneven gal's heart. I can't stop thinking about it," she said, stopping on the first step. "There's just one thing I'm afraid of..."

"I know... I know. Mortgage rates are up, but they say it's going to get even worse. Ten percent by next year, I reckon. We ought to strike while the iron's hot before it sizzles our pocketbook to a char."

"No, that's not it," she said, shaking her head and rolling her eyes. "You know my old boss lived there a while. I just feel weird even considering it, given his... disappearance."

"You afraid of a ghost? Come on, Nancy. Grow up."

"No! I'm afraid of bankruptcy because my screw-up for a husband can't keep a job."

Ron remained cool and collected despite the jab. "You've been plagued by worse thoughts, haven't you? Cope with it. Water off a duck's back, right?" he said, shucking his hand across her shoulder.

"Thanks for your sincerity, jackass." She jabbed him in the ribs as they moved toward the door. Her face animated as she looked toward Ron. She screamed. "The door's forced open..."

"Way to give us away, Nancy! Step back. Stay quiet. I'm gonna grab my pistol."

He jogged toward the vehicle, grabbing his .38 *Smith and Wesson*. Returning to the steps, he put his finger over his lips, holding the revolver close to his side.

"What's going on here?" he yelled, flicking the light on. "I've got a gun!"

Idiot thinks he can just come in and play Wyatt Earp, she thought. *What if they're still here? What if there's more than one? Think before you act, dummy!*

Ron came back around the corner just outside the front door, standing next to Nancy to give the potential intruders a chance to make themselves known.

"Nancy, you look upstairs," he groveled. "I'll look down here."

She shook her head. "I'm not coming inside until *you* make sure the house is safe. You're the one with the gun, remember?"

Breathe in... breathe out...

"You don't care about him at all, do you?" he asked, shaking the gun in the sky as the pitter patter of the nighttime rain hit the porch rooftop. "Get in. I'll shoot 'em if there's anyone that shouldn't be in here. They could come up behind us outside, too. You never know."

"Ron, stop it, now. You go first. I'll follow behind. Chivalry's not dead yet, is it?"

"Shut up," he mumbled, his teeth gritted together.

Running through the house, he searched feverishly for their son.

"Get in," he yelled.

Fine. I'm coming.

Nancy went inside, careful not to make much noise. After checking two of the upstairs bedrooms and noticing them unscathed, she opened the hall closet door. Randy's new babysitter was bound, gagged, and lying on the floor with electrical tape wrapped tightly around her head and covering her entire face; her chest heaving up and down.

"Ron, get up here," she yelled. "Mackenzie's tied up in the closet."

"I'm still looking for Randy," he called from below. "He might be down here. Can't you handle it?"

"Get your butt up here! She could be seriously hurt." She grabbed a pair of scissors from her craft supply box, cutting through the rope.

"What about our boy?" Ron yelled from below. "Don't you care? What kind of mother are you?"

"Ron, we don't know where he is. Let's prioritize what we know. Mackenzie might have answers," she said, unraveling the tape from the trembling babysitter's face. Her beautiful dark hair was scalped in various places — her brows stripped away from the tension of the tape as it was removed. Nancy distributed Mackenzie's hair around as best as possible to cover up the spots where it appeared left thin.

"Ms. Nancy, I'm so... sorry," Mackenzie said, short on breath, and trying to sit up. "They go... they got Randy."

"Who? Why?" she said, her voice escalating.

Mackenzie shook her head. "I no know. It happened so fast..."

"You're sure they got him?" she asked, her breath matching Mackenzie's.

Ron stormed up the stairs. "Nancy, I don't know where he is," he grabbed the back of his head with both hands. "Holy cow! Mackenzie, what happened to you? Where's Randy?"

"Ron, don't patronize her. Go take a panic pill. She was part of this invasion too," Nancy said, stroking her fingers through Mackenzie's hair.

"The house is as clean as when we left it," he said. "I can't think of anyone else that would want to disrupt our lives this way. Can you?"

She looked away as the glowing eyes of Creeper Joe flashed in front of her. "No. Anyone I'd be concerned with is as good as dead."

They walked downstairs, seating Mackenzie on the plaid-printed couch.

"We'll get you some help, honey," Nancy said. "Wait here. I'm so sorry."

"Ms. Nancy, I'm sorry. I should no answer the door. They rang and I answer while I was on phone. It was local call, I swear you."

"Did you recognize them?" Ron asked, his voice growing louder. "What implored you to answer the door? We told you not to. Have you seen this neighborhood? We're not destitute, but the area's not crime free, either."

"No, Mr. Ron." Her eyes teared up, and her voice remained shaky. "She was older. It was raining. I thought she might need help. You no picture old lady committing this kind of crime. Mama says it's always the men just like on the TV."

"Mackenzie, it's the nineties," Ron said. "Anything could happen. We got *Fatal Attraction* chicks around here these days."

Nancy glared at Ron, her eyes jagged daggers.

What's going through your head, brainless?

"Ron, get in the kitchen. We need to make a plan, rather than prolong this discussion any further."

He scoffed, his voice growing sarcastic, mimicking Nancy. "Wait, 'Mackenzie might have answers,' right?"

Tears ran down her cheeks. "I'm calling the cops. Dear God, I hope he's not dead!" she said, grabbing the telephone.

Ron threw his fist on the kitchen counter. "Nancy, don't do anything stupid! I'm not ready for *them* to be notified. Some of these guys are crooked. If you're not inbred with the right family or from the right clan, you're as good as useless. You should know that by now!"

Of course I do. Just give me a minute.

"What are you talking about?" she asked, scratching at her arm anxiously. "Why don't you want them coming? Do you have something to confess? Are you brushing elbows with that drug-dealing punk from the Gas 'n Sip again?"

He shook his head, trembling.

"Tell me now," she said, "before we both end up dead."

"It's not like that, Nancy." He took one of his panic pills from the upper cabinet. "Those days are long behind me. I swear."

"Tch. Long behind you? How long's it been? Six months, right? As many years as you've logged, I don't understand how you can be so generic with time."

He fidgeted with the paper towel roller. "I'm just... not trusting the local authorities. We can't trust anyone. Fix me a glass of ice water, would you?"

I'll fix you a can of whoop ass. How about that?

"Anything else, your highness?" she asked. "How can you think about *your* needs at such a delicate time?"

"These things happen."

"Is that all you can say? Sheesh, Ron, how fast does that stuff work? Your medication mellowing you out this much may not be a good thing. I liked the cowboy that came in the house earlier with his gun when we saw the door forced open. Randy's missing... Come up with a plan!"

Mackenzie came into the room. "I'm sorry to interrupt, Mr. Ron... Ms. Nancy... Mama's here. I go home, now."

"Dear God, we let the time slip away," Nancy said.

Ron spoke to Mackenzie, "Here's your money. Can I ask you a favor? Don't tell your mom about Randy. Ms. Nancy and I will look into this further."

"No money... I take no money. What good is babysitter if kid goes missing?" she said, tears streaming down her cheeks.

"It's not completely your fault, sweetheart. Just take the money," Nancy said softly, rubbing her on the shoulder.

"I go to mom's car," Mackenzie replied, wiping the lingering tears from her eyes.

"What about your eyebrows? Those parts of your hair that are missing," Ron said. "They're gone!"

"No worry, Mr. Ron... we draw on eyebrows. Mama and I use scalp concealer for thin spots, anyway. I say prayer you find him. I won't tell her. I know she will freak out on me."

Mackenzie walked out of the house, waving toward them.

"That was a casual exit. You sure she's not gonna go to the cops?" Ron asked, staring Nancy down intently.

"We paid her well, didn't we?" she muttered.

"I don't think an extra twenty bucks is enough to keep her quiet with a scarred memory," Ron said.

"Nothing was missing," she muttered.

"Nothing but Randy? Our entire world is missing, Nancy! Come on!"

"Well, we aren't worth that much, so a ransom seems out of the question..."

"Ransom? You assume he's alive. We've got to retrace our steps."

"Okay, then. Let's play detective..." she said.

He grabbed her on the shoulder. "Why are *you* so melancholy? We're talking about our child, here! She said something about an older lady. Let's think simpler. Who do we know? Maybe your mom just got wasted and came and picked him up. The broad's done that kind of thing before, right? She's always been a bit... unconventional... and jealous. Seeing Mackenzie babysit Randy may have brought out that tinge of inner racist in her from growing up in the twenties and thirties."

"Maybe so," she said, sighing and staring through the kitchen window.

Stroke his ego. He might come to a smarter conclusion.

"Mackenzie was bound and gagged," she said. "If it was mom that did that... I swear..."

He looked at Nancy, his face growing pale.

No amount of medication can fix him. Can it?

"The orange jumpsuit might match her skin tone and accentuate her figure pretty well," she said shakily. "You never know."

"Nancy, this is no time to joke. "

She shook her head. "You know how I feel about her. You call her yourself if you think *your* idea is an actual possibility. I think you're just buzzed from dinner."

Ron chuckled. "You're probably right. How about that glass of water?"

"How about I sock you in the eye? How would that be? Selfish pig."

She pulled the freezer door open. Peering inside, she shrieked. Despite her volume, Ron remained calm and approached her. She hoisted two Ziploc bags of hair in the air.

"It looks like Randy's red hair in this baggie," she said, sniffling twice. "I'll bet it's Mackenzie's in the other, along with a small piece of her scalp connected to it."

Ron's eyes narrowed. "Hey. What's that at the bottom of the bag?"

She pulled the extra piece out. "Ugh... it's more skin. What the hell is going on?"

Magazine clippings of various words were distributed across a sheet of olive-toned skin.

Locks of love... and lots of pain. Who is the one that's going insane? I'll give you a hint. I ain't hellbent. Just know... you better stay away!

SUMMER 1991

CHAPTER FIVE

NANCY HELBENS sat down with her new manager, Jerry Greenwich — a burned out hotel man who wore out the seams of his pants at an overnight chain across town, got laid off, and found his way back into success by kissing the right legislator's ass. The end result, the Oak Hollow Hotel was zoned historically significant.

Randy's disappearance remained a problem, but holding down a job and remaining away from home seemed the best approach to diverting her inner turmoil. She hoped the paycheck and associated creature comforts would meet the need.

Alright, First Day! Let's get things moving.

The basement office in the restored iteration of the hotel remained uninteresting to Nancy. Despite her past traumas and memories associated with the building, a growing numbness toward her current state of affairs left her anxiety over the troubled hotel abnormally minimal and indifferent. If anything, she convinced herself the place shielded her in unexplainable ways.

She looked around the room, studying a couple of cheap bookshelves lining either wall, a few pictures of the hotel and its 1926 ribbon cutting — side by side with the January 1991 reopening, and Greenwich's purple coffee mug on the edge of the desk. The window looked into the dark tunnel that ran behind it, shrouded by a set of matching aquamarine curtains that were more of a monstrosity than any kind of compliment to the room.

What's the point of a window in the basement?

The tone-deaf Greenwich must have also been color blind. His monotone voice was such that Nancy could only pay attention for brief intervals before drifting away.

"The job is a good fit for me, sir. This building and I are acquainted."

Greenwich swooped his razor thin hair across the top of his round head as a bead of perspiration dripped into his coffee. "I understand that, but don't let that overconfidence give you too much solace. I saw the interviews. The way you exploited the media with your story. Little details don't add up, Nancy. Most people never notice, but the funny thing about lying is, the truth always has a way of seeping out, whether you want it to or not." His voice faded into a garble. After about fifteen seconds, he clapped his hands to get her attention. "Did you tune me out or what? I need you listening if you're going to work here."

Nancy began sweating as the lamp above put off an excessive amount of heat. She dabbed her forehead with the side of her arm, looking up at the light.

"It's a heat lamp," he said. "The basement stays ten degrees cooler than I want it to. You know the rules of the house preclude both of us, so I won't bore you with details. Listen up, though. It's essential we do our best to ensure that the hotel is managed well... and with care. I want you to understand the importance of your role. The hospitality business is pretty stable, but the boutique niche of vintage hotel restorations is still a pipedream in Riverton. Once word gets out, we'll be occupied every night, but, the times we're not, you needn't worry. The place will never leave you hanging — if you take care of it right."

He slammed a dusty book on the table top. "This is the hotel policy manual... dreamed up and put together by its original founder, my mother's cousin, Don Wasserman. I couldn't tell you much about it, other than that it was recovered in the basement just twenty-five feet from where we're sitting now. After the fire..."

BLAH. BLAH. BLAH. What do you need from me?

"Thanks for the information." Her paperthin impatience came through in her speech. "Show me... don't tell me. What do I do with this?"

"Don't get cheeky with me, lady." He put his hand on the top of hers — his sweaty, chunky palms making her skin crawl. "Learn it like the back of your hand — every last crease and freckle." His ugly grin made her throat sink.

Nancy peered through the small crevice between the curtains as Greenwich continued to mumble away about the hotel. She should have been more enchanted with the stories but found her mind wandering back to Mackenzie and Randy, the note left behind, and the unconventional means with which it was crafted — doing her best to preserve spending emotions on the event or Randy's whereabouts.

A fiery glow flickered between the curtains. A woman's cackling laugh resonated just behind as she danced around a glowing firepit in a gray smock.

God help me, she thought.

Though only catching glimpses of the peculiar ritual, Nancy grew pale and motionless. It had been too long. She could see the weak glow shining through the woman's eyes as she further showed off graceful movements in her superficial youth. Her breathy voice chilled the tunnel as a repetitive chant flowed through her at what seemed an inhuman and unfamiliar rhythm.

I remember that chant. I don't want to...

As the voice grew louder, Greenwich's did the same in what seemed an effort to distract Nancy. "Let's finish this discussion in the lobby, please." He motioned her toward the door. "You seem more concerned with my tenant in the tunnel than with the job I'm paying you for."

She shook her head, her growing frustrations erupting. "What's going on here? What is *she* doing?" She walked toward the window before Greenwich cut her off.

"Not a step further or you won't be working here any longer. I don't see her as relevant to our discussion," he said.

"And why is that?" she asked.

WHAP!

He rubber-stamped a sheet, adjusting some paperwork on top of his desk and later proceeding to show her out the door. "The tunnel behind my office is being leased by a local artist. She's around often. Here lately, her boy's been around, too. Matter of fact, years ago, she was a substitute art teacher at the high school. I hadn't seen her in a good while. I could swear she hasn't aged a day since then. If I did the math right, I'm impressed she's still of childbearing age. I wish I had that kind of vitality coursing through my veins."

"Huh? Substitute? She seems a bit on the eccentric side," Nancy said.

"Eccentric, yes. Even a smidgen pagan, but she pays her rent on time. I struggle to say anything negative about her... or about her kid. We were well acquainted in the past — if you know what I mean." He raised his caterpillar eyebrows up and down. "When the time is appropriate, I'll introduce you. Until then, get in the lobby and learn that policy manual. Will you?"

"That's unnecessary. I'm not that eager to... meet another pagan. I thought you had something else you wanted to discuss."

They walked up the stairs into the lobby. Greenwich's hefty feet clunked up the steps as if they were filled with lead weights — his own breath elevating by the third step.

He stayed a couple of steps behind her, peering up from below. "That's a nice dress you're wearing. What I have to say... it's something I'm not sure you're ready to hear."

"Get your bug eyes off my big ass. Will ya?" she muttered.

He huffed as he reached the top step. "I'm sorry. What was that?"

"Nothing. What am I not ready to hear?" She rested her hand on her hip as they both caught their breath.

Greenwich smiled at her. "I keep the Reese's peanut butter cups in the galley. I figured you might appreciate knowing that."

Nancy studied Greenwich's face for a few seconds. "How did you know about that?"

He laughed at her, his smug grin interrupted with the perspiration that dripped from his forehead. "It's not rocket science, Nancy. You had a smudge of chocolate next to your lip, a lump of peanut butter between your teeth, and I saw the wrappers in the dashboard of your vehicle when you drove up. I know you're not a slob, but when a kid tires on us for a while, we all get a little laxed with our tidiness. That's okay."

"I said nothing about *him*. Why are you bringing my son up? He's my business and no one else's. You got it?"

"Gah," he said, shaking his head. "No need to get testy, ginger. I was just trying to make chit-chat."

She scoffed. "Tch. Stop, now."

He walked her around the hotel lobby. It was vaster and more open than it had been in years past. The natural light from the outside gave it a life that had long been choked away from it. There were impressive fixtures, elaborate doorways, lavish seating arrangements, and an information center full of pamphlets, offering guests the finest in regional cuisines, activities, and libations. Each of the large room's curtains were carefully draped, covering portions of the lobby windows in a beautiful fuchsia-colored fabric as the afternoon sunshine peeked through.

The entire space was drenched in art deco influence, a taste of the success story once planned for it years earlier. The lobby ceilings featured multicolored patterns that were a struggle for eyes to follow or study, but nonetheless, charming curb appeals to first-time guests. The contrast was offset by brilliant crimson red walls and white stripes, and a checkered floor pattern that often disoriented the buzzed and intoxicated upon arrival. The circular benches strewn about the lobby space featured well placed ficus trees in their center and other artificial plants — green year-round without a drop of water. The doors to other areas in the lobby were a beautiful antique wood finish with oblong frosty glass panels. In contrast to much of the rest, a large painting of William Wasserman stood in the corner in honor of the father of the hotel's fallen founder, Don.

Greenwich mumbled to Nancy, "Yeah. The lobby fountains draw currency from guests like wishing wells. You'll be fishing those coins out weekly. Sometimes, we'll get a peso or a pound sterling, even Canadian quarters... It's no problem with me if you want to keep 'em to give to the boy or waste a few of the American coins in a vending machine on yourself now and then."

The bar in the lobby's northwest corner had not employed a bartender. It merely sat there, empty and catching dust. Wine glasses dangled from the cut outs as a large mirror struggled to flatter either of their figures.

Greenwich studied Nancy. His overreaching gaze was discomforting, like a lingering worm that would not stop pestering until he found his way back to play in the dirt beneath.

He motioned all around the room. "It's bustling with life. Isn't it?"

"Well, in a manner of speaking," she said softly. "Hopefully it'll be chock full of people one of these days so our pockets can go deeper."

He rested his sausage fingers across her shoulder. "It's always chock full of people, Nancy. You just need to change your perspective, that's all. See the world through the lenses God gave you. The potential... half full is always better than half empty. You get it?" He lifted his hand from her shoulder and pointed to the revolving doorway. "Looks like a customer's coming in now. Get to it."

I feel his sweat running down my shoulder. Ugh.

"Yes, sir. I'll speak to you later."

Get out of here, creep, she thought. *Why does every man feel the need to hit on me? I just want to live a day uninterrupted. Is that so much to ask?*

***

Less than an hour later, Greenwich fumbled his way back into the lobby.

"Nancy, I've watched you on the surveillance cameras. You've been doing a good job playing house and taking care of things. I'm going to ask you a personal question."

Good gracious, she thought. *What are you going to ask...?*

"Okay?" she said, closing her eyes an extra second. "Yeah, go ahead."

"I should have told you before, but, after today, I need you to work the overnight shift. The other guy just gave his notice. Another casualty to the dad-gum chain hotel phenomenon across town. They're damn snakes, snatching up our people one by one, and lighting up the skies of Riverton with their colorful and familiar logos."

Maybe the pay's better.

She gulped. "Overnight?"

"Yes. I'll arrange for you to have a place to retreat to in the basement for the latter part of the shift during the quieter hours, and you'll just go on call. We can put the hotel on autopilot for a while each night. It's not that big a thing."

Nancy sighed, rubbing her forehead. "As I mentioned, sir, my household responsibilities and my role as a parent may be a setback. This won't be easy."

"The boy can stay if and when he needs to — as long as he doesn't trash the place. It's not any big deal. On second thought, maybe you can make your husband watch him now and then."

"I've tried." She pulled her hair into a ponytail. "I don't think it's in his DNA. I'm hoping the hotel bar is stocked with something heavier than complimentary orange juice."

"Ha-ha. It's not. What do you mean?" he asked, his cheeky smile enough to make her cringe.

"He's a goof. I've lost all hope."

Greenwich tightened his belt loop a notch, struggling to suck his gut in. "On behalf of my kind, let me be the first to apologize."

Nancy studied him. His greasy face reeked of a man only moderately more refined than Ron and no less nuanced with quirks.

"Don't worry about it. It's getting complicated with Randy, though. Ron's got an apartment he leased out. Our house has been on the lonely side. It's an adjustment for all of us."

"Well, take it as a sign. You can just move into one of the basement apartments here. I'm sure it will help y'all save a few bucks. I'm no expert at patching up crap marriages, but you can't blame me for trying. As long as you're employed here, you have a home. Make it right by me, though. Don't you dare take advantage."

She found her seat at the lobby desk. "I won't. Thank you, sir. Give me some time to think it over."

Greenwich bit his lip, saying, "I need an answer now. Someone's got to cover the shift tonight and I simply refuse to do it."

What a selfish man, she thought. *Going to leave a woman in harm's way.*

"What about overnight security? Would a man not be more suited for these hours?"

Greenwich rubbed the back of his neck. "Liberate yourself, Nancy. I would have thought you were some kind of feminist. You don't need to depend on a man. Besides, I've installed a locking system that either of us can trigger. There's a hidden panel on the back wall. The locks are on a timer unless they're opened from the inside. Just be discreet. We don't need every Tom, Dick, and Harry knowing where it is."

He walked toward it, giving her a quick demonstration.

"Okay. So, you're asking me to start tonight?" she asked.

"I've already said that. It's what needs to happen, Nancy. Is that okay?"

"Alright, fine. How about a raise for working these hours?"

Greenwich smiled at her. "How about continental breakfast, a room, and free local calling?"

"Well said," she replied. "I can't argue with that. Anything else?"

He tucked his shirt back into the front of his pants. "No visitors after 2AM. Believe you me, you'll have the men swooning over you in a heartbeat when they see you yank that dimestore rock off your hand."

Dimestore rock... these are real diamonds... or at least, Ron told me they were.

"Alright. Randy's not an issue yet. He's out-of-town staying with his granddad," she lied, her eyes drifting away from Greenwich for a second.

He swooped the lingering hairs across the top of his bald scalp after licking his fingertips. "You're hopeless. Men say they can change, but we just don't. We're nothing more than pre-programmed slugs returning to old habits the first damn chance we get. Start tonight. I'll make it worth your while on that first paycheck. Okay?"

What does that mean—make it worth my while? Five cents more per hour? A new pillowtop mattress? Free cable TV in my room?

"Yes, sir."

"If you need anything. You know what to do."

"Yes. Always check the policy manual first. If I can't find an answer, then come to you for help."

"That's what I'm paying you for. Get to it," he said, walking toward the basement. The loose change and keys jingled in his pockets as his feet pounded across the floor.

CHAPTER SIX

VIC RAMSEY found his way into the Corner Brothers Deli — a hole in the wall two blocks from old Town Riverton and one of three stops he had yet to make in the area.

He pulled out his pad and began to write. It was nondescript, but a glimpse into his thoughts, which might prove interesting to Dorse and his growing entourage of readers.

I won't give up. That's not my way. A hit piece on the chain restaurants would be a waste of time. What's the best I'm going to come up with? Meth being served out the drive-thru window? A manager and a fry cook in the back office getting it on? Come on! Bore me to tears, will you? That kind of filler will land me at the Anvil. On behalf of my previous columns, let me be the first to say, ladies and germs, this is the dawn of a new day. I won't be subjecting you to hit pieces on the second-rate pubs, restaurants, and bars anymore. Instead, I'll be discovering my roots. The place I want to be. Where is that, you ask? Writing to you like you were sitting right next to me. I'm thankful for the opportunity, and hungry to deliver better. Transforming a column will take a lot of work. Transforming a newspaper will take an act of God. To my editor, Hal Dorse, I'm sorry when I got carried away before. Columnists, writers, editors, we can all get a big ego. Next thing you know, we're convinced we're in line for a Pulitzer, and then, reality sets in. We're one step from mediocrity and a cardiac arrest away from being dead and buried. I choose to push myself — further and further. If it costs me anything, the release I feel is worth it. The transparency is refreshing, and I hope it is for you. All of you burned out investment bankers, government workers, and lawyers out there, it's time to get your priorities straight. Don't blink your eyes too fast. Your children will be grown up and gone before you know it. Is the quest for cash worth missing your son's baseball game and your daughter's dance recital? They won't ever forget when you miss it. Here's to new beginnings and to a future that's bright with potential. I will return you back to your scheduled broadcasting in a forthcoming column as I move into the miscellaneous metro section. Riverton's got more to uncover and I want to keep my finger on the pulse to deliver it to you with a flavor and zest you'll grow to appreciate like a fine wine. Ambition will advance us, but only experience can grow us.

    -VR

He dropped his black-inked Bic on the table, running his fingers through his graying hair.

Not a bad little blip, Ramsey, he thought. *String together a few more coherent thoughts and you might be onto something.*

Free-form writing for the *Statesman* gave him a taste of the youthful ambition he carried years earlier when his writing was a mere hobby. The open floor plan to the restaurant was cozy but bright as the workers jabbered away behind the counter.

Dorse is right, he thought. *I need to spice things up. Where the heck am I going with life? What's my purpose? A lot of experience and a moderately impressive resume of accolades and titles, but it all feels meaningless in the moment. I'm due a change of pace.*

He sipped on his styrofoam cup of unsweet tea, biting into his sandwich. The toasted ham and cheese had grown cold.

Ugh... this stuff isn't that great. Maybe I will write up an article on this joint.

Standing up, he threw away his leftovers and walked out of the restaurant, leaving an unnecessary five-dollar bill on the table as he waved to the cashier. He brushed elbows with a short woman, carrying a paperback as she entered. They made eye contact, and he smiled at her.

All hope is not lost — still some cute ones floating around, he thought.

He walked out at a chipper pace. "Have a good day, ma'am."

She glared back as if he were a foreigner.

CHAPTER SEVEN

NANCY HELBENS dined at the Corner Brothers Deli with a cozy mystery paperback in her hands while she sipped on the potato soup. She dipped her toasted turkey club in the soup between pages, enjoying a culmination of the two together – until she arrived to the stale unsweet tea. Its more popular counterpart was not an item at Corner Brothers. The Corner Brothers eccentric management refused to relent on stocking the southern favorite, despite Nancy's recurring complaints.

Not enough counter space, my ass. Make the damn sweet tea!

The northwest corner booth was an incredible escape for Nancy. She woke an hour past twelve after sleeping off the night shift in her hotel basement quarters. The shifts were supposed to be twelve hours, the final three, on-call, with a "Ring Bell for Service" placard placed on the counter from 2-5AM and a sophisticated hotel buzzer system on the outside to screen guests in during these hours. Only the clerk or Greenwich could reply. Greenwich's sleep patterns were irregular and unpredictable, leaving Nancy the primary party responsible for the overnight vetting process. Bizarre characters trickled through the adjacent Old Town Riverton and Oak Hollow Districts from time to time, but rarely posed much of a threat.

Wrapping up her chapter, she placed the book face down as the ding of the restaurant's front door caught her attention. She knew the face, but she wasn't ready for a conversation. She had not seen Livewire in a handful of years. His hair was shorter, his face slimmer, his eyes redder. She studied him a moment, before sliding in her seat a little lower, and hoping he would miss her entirely.

Her chestnut bangs were different, her face cuter and dolled up after a lot of constructive feedback from Ron. The lectures on how a woman might be prim and proper in public had dulled with time, leading her to further abandon her mother's overbearing, all-natural approach. She was a reinvented woman. The slew of oral surgeries and well-suited veneers were a drastic improvement to her questionable dental hygiene practices of yesteryear — her pockets full of breath mints, a saving grace to herself and anyone else that spent extended amounts of time with her. True self-confidence had taken much discipline but always remained reachable.

As Livewire ordered at the counter, Nancy momentarily recalled her desires for a deeper relationship with him in the past, but their unnatural union in the tunnel left her feelings in a swirl — her heartstrings wanderlust. The sound of two quarters hit the counter as he carried his cup to the coffee dispenser. A mere twenty-five feet from her on the black-and-white checkered flooring stood the missing piece of her heart before Ron.

His dress code remained the same, the black shirt and black jeans fresher than she remembered, and the keys in his oversized pockets jingling as he approached the table next to hers. He sat down, wiping his Lennon inspired frames. As he put them back on, his eyes widened when he made eye contact with Nancy sitting to his right.

"Oh my gosh... Nancy Helbens? Is that you?" he asked, standing up from the table, his peepers aglow.

Don't look so excited about how pretty I am now with hair and makeup, she thought. *How bad was I before, seriously?*

Trying to seem shy and bashful, she looked away for a moment. "Yes. Come have a seat with me. I'm by myself."

He studied her as he moved across to the booth. "You look extraordinary."

"And I should." She pointed to the gaudy rock on her finger.

He sipped his coffee. "What else is new? The last time I saw you..." He stopped, inhaling air through his teeth. "I'm just going to say it, right here and right now. We made a pact."

"We did," she said, looking away at the blank wall.

He twisted his coffee cup around in circles, hesitating to continue the conversation topic, "You didn't keep it. I still have a television, Nancy. How have the payouts been? Was your exaggerated story worth it? One second in the public eye wasn't enough for you, was it? You had to have two or three, didn't ya?"

She took her last bite of sandwich, chewing a second before she responded. "Not as good as you would think. They found out more about me, my political affiliations, my religion, blah, blah, blah. Next thing you know, they kicked me to the curb. I didn't fit their mold as an ideal victim. I'm not a pretty blonde bimbo with deep pockets and big bosoms. I'm an average Mary Jane from the wrong side of the tracks. No amount of studio make-up or theatrics can make up for that. I am what I am."

He smiled. "I appreciate your honesty with me. It's all overrated, anyhow. Weren't you afraid of what might happen to you? That someone might come after you when you started spillin' the beans?"

"For a while," she said, crumpling up her sandwich paper and bag of potato chips. "At some point, I stopped worrying about it and decided I was ready to be made whole again."

He finished his coffee. "To be made whole again? I swear to heaven if my family could ever 'be made whole' again, I'd give a kidney."

"Why can't it? We all have a chance to prosper. We just have to work hard for it, right?"

"It doesn't matter, Nancy. My past is a footnote I'd rather not discuss... So, tell me about your marriage? How's that going? Any kids?"

She looked at the floor. "Well... we have our boy, Randy. I guess there are two kids, if you count my husband, Ron. Almost fifty years old and still not sure what to do with his life."

"Why bother, then? Cute gal like you can do pretty well for yourself when you put in some extra elbow grease."

You're so sincere, she thought. *Jerk.*

"I was looking for a path to a better life," she said. "Revisiting my past uncovers too much I don't want to relive again. What's new with you?"

"Not much. Still divorced, single, wirin' buildings... you know, chasin' the dream."

"What is your dream?" she asked.

"You said it already, Nancy. To be made whole again. I've got to run. I don't need to meddle in your affairs too long, anyhow. You've got a family to prioritize. It's great to see you. May the spirits guide your heart where it belongs."

He stood up, pitched his cup in the garbage bin, and walked out of the restaurant.

It's great to see you, too. What am I doing with my life?

***

On her way home, she walked past the abandoned WGBO station building, remembering back to when she and Ron first became an item. Then, there was Randy's arrival, a nine-month engagement, and a fast track into marriage.

What was it about him that swooned me over? He was always eccentric... I guess he was convenient. I wasn't getting younger or slimmer, either. I wanted to prove to mom I could do better than her and raise my children right.

Studying the building a moment too long, Johnny Lathrop drove up beside her in his beat-up blue Cutlass Ciera. He jammed his cigarette on the dash, swatting the smoke away as he rolled the window a couple of notches.

"Hey, Nancy, right?" he called out.

Crap, not this guy again.

She sighed. "Yeah... that's me."

His eyes lit up as he rattled out words at the speed of a heavily caffeinated auctioneer, "Are you in the market for commercial real estate? This place is going for a real bargain. I could see an entrepreneurial spirit in your eyes when we met the other day. Maybe a fine women's boutique... or a nice gallery?"

Nancy scoffed. "How about a liquor store and a sign that says buzz off?"

He puckered his lips. "Sheesh, lady. I get the message. Call me if you're still interested in that house or this lot. Oh... and tell Ron I said hi."

"We're separated. I booted his miserable ass across town last week." She turned away, continuing to walk toward the car.

"I know, but you've got the kid, right? You can still send regards from his favorite real estate guy. I got him into that apartment, by the way. Take care. Call me if you get lonely."

Alright, get on. Creep.

CHAPTER EIGHT

VIC RAMSEY studied his manager's uncomfortable body language. The corner office of senior Statesman editor, Hal Dorse, was simple. A lone touch toned telephone stood atop the walnut desk next to his electric Olympia typewriter. To his right, sat a table with recent publications triaged for review. A pack of Lucky Strike cigarettes sat on the corner of the desk nearest him, while he kept a smoke tucked behind his right ear in line for his next drag.

Look at you... sitting confidently in your little leather swivel chair, convinced you've got it all figured out. What do you have that I don't? A superficial degree mounted on your wall? Baggage from an extra divorce? A thicker head of hair? Come on!

Dorse's annoying voice bothered Vic, almost to the point of quitting. It was difficult not to picture his five-nine superior more like a cartoon character with exaggerated features. The cleft in his chin, the toilet paper pieces where he cut himself shaving, and the beady eyes — the problems went on and on. Even his simple name perturbed Ramsey.

On quieter days, Vic sketched him into a doodle, hopeful that his second-rate cartoon character would not be recovered by the overnight cleaning crew after he left for the day.

"I've already nudged you once. Do a follow up on the hotel. Pick up where Calhoun left off," Dorse said. "It's been months since... since the fiascos. I hear they replaced the elevator. I'll give you one more shot, Ramsey. If you screw this up, we'll be going our separate ways. You get it? I've let you freewheel for a while, and you probably picked up a few readers, but you've pissed off even more. Blabbering editorials from uneducated philosophers don't sell papers. Headlines do." Dorse stood up from his desk as if to shoe him out. "I've got better things to do than babysit an overrated hack attracted to shock factor hit pieces and misplaced lingo. You swore to me you were a pro at prose but somehow, as each day passes by and I study your work closer, it speaks of sloppy — a man desperate to find his identity. An extension on another contract with the *Statesman* may not be in your future. Calhoun dulled with every article he wrote, too—like some kind of spark dwindling to the end, a ticking timebomb. Don't let history repeat itself. Riverton's an interesting town. You've been over there. Old Town and Oak Hollow are areas with all kinds of spooks and kooks you would fit in just fine with."

I guess we're finished here, he thought. *Don't get smart.*

"You know what, Dorse? You're right. I'll get over there... soon. Let me scribble some notes and see what else I can come up with. Just you wait, there's always the possibility this... hack will leave you shell-shocked and selling a boatload of papers."

Dorse chuckled softly before sipping his coffee. The red mug cast a notable red glow on his face. "Lots of talk and never any action. Get your scrawny ass over there and prove me wrong."

"Give me a week or two and I'll take a stab at it. It's still too soon..."

***

Later that afternoon, he left his article on Dorse's desk. The office stood empty with the lingering stench of his final cigarette in the ashtray; its remnants left behind. The receptionist mentioned to Vic that he left early for the day, feeling under the weather. As Vic made his way home, he stopped by the city cemetery to visit his parents' shared grave, a double-spaced plot for an uncommon doublewide casket. His grandfather's headstone stood just behind. Though he felt short-changed by their untimely exit and the conversations they never shared, he idealized them in his memory like any "color inside the lines" type would.

Trying to live with no regrets, dad, he thought.

His chest pounded as he tapped on the top of the gravestone, overwhelmed by the emotion of staying close by a moment too long. Sitting down and pulling out one of his nitro pills, he popped it in his mouth.

So dry... breathe, Ramsey. Breathe. You overdid it on the coffee again. It's two minutes. Hold on... Not good for a weak heart. You know that.

Floaters ran across the fronts of his eyes as the blue sky washed away into a haze. His father stared down at him, hovering just above. He stood covered in blood and glass from the accident. Just the way Vic remembered him at the scene before they pronounced his old man dead.

"It's okay," his father said. "It's not your time, son. Hold on..."

"If it's not my time, why am I seeing you? You've been gone a long while, dad."

"It's just your subconscious, fighting with everything it has to keep you vital," his father answered, pulling out the shards of glass from his skin, one after the next as the wounds closed up and healed.

Vic reached toward him. "I just want one more cold drink with you. One more chat. I never got the closure I wanted."

"We didn't end on bad terms, did we, son? It was just one of those things. I hate that you're carrying guilt, but I don't resent you for it. Our moment together will come in due time, Vic. It's just too soon. I'm proud of you."

Vic's heart relaxed. He sat up as a cemetery caretaker walked by in overalls and a green t-shirt.

"I th...thought I was going to have to d...dig you a plot, mister. Ain't never seen a m...man die in a c...cemetery before."

Vic smiled at the young man as color restored in his face and his breathing normalized. "It was close, but apparently the saints haven't called me home just yet."

The stuttering caretaker shuffled backwards. "I c... c... could have sworn I'd seen a ghost. You were p...paler than a bleached bedsheet."

Vic stood up and waved. "I guess I better get going. It's nice to see someone taking a moment to check on another for a change. I was beginning to think people like that didn't exist anymore."

"No, s...sir. You're still flesh and blood to me. Way b...better than whatever psycho keeps coming out and d...digging my graves up."

Now that's interesting... and not something you hear about every day.

"What was that, partner?" Vic asked, brushing off the grass and dirt from his slacks.

"I'm not allowed to t...talk about it. I could get f...f... freaking fired," he muttered, looking over his shoulder.

"Why?"

"I'm sorry, mister. Th...that's it."

"No, no. I'm a reporter, and this is juicy. We have some grave robbing going on?"

The caretaker's fidgeting left Vic watching him closer.

"Mister, I app...appreciate what you do and all," he stammered, "but I s...swear if I'm found out as the source of this in...information, I'll be in a p...plot six feet under with the r...rest."

Vic nodded his head, shaking hands with the young caretaker. "I understand. I'm sorry to press you. I'll do my research on it. Take care, now. Thanks for what you do. I know it's bound to be an unappreciated job. Thankless work is often the hardest."

The caretaker's face showed no emotion. "Be c...c...careful. No man should l...linger in a graveyard after dark."

Vic walked out of the cemetery, continuing toward his Impala.

Driving across town, he pondered upon the comments of the caretaker.

I'll go loiter around Bridgewater for a drink a while and go back. Maybe I'll stumble across something interesting. Dorse would eat this story up. It might even be a ticket to another extension on my contract with the Statesman.

CHAPTER NINE

Entering the Bridgewater Restaurant, VIC RAMSEY moved toward the bar. It was his first trip into the storied restaurant. While his mind wandered about the angle to take his next article, the hum of the room grew duller and duller while the light up Flitz beer sign buzzed and flickered. The laughter of the fellow diners and drinkers faded to silence as he closed his eyes.

It's going to have to be cutthroat. Low blows and rabbit punches permitted.

Looking around the room, he studied the bald bartender peering back at him, a growing look of frustration having come over the man.

His mind wandered. *Who's going to make the first move... you or me? You work here. You greet me!*

The bartender's voice rattled Vic from the first word. "Are you going to order something... or just take up space at my bar? I work on tips."

The sarcasm in his mind ran wild. *Is sounding like an old movie mobster part of your shtick. Or, are you really from Little Italy?*

"Fine... fine. I'll take a splash of *Old Tymer's* in an ice-cold glass. Mix it up with a cola, would you?"

"Whatever you say, man," the bartender said, rolling his eyes, and turning around to make the drink.

Man? Who do you think I am?

Vic looked around the room as the surrounding chatter continued. Sitting by himself was never a bother. He worked better that way. In his perfect world, TV dinners, to-go meals, and soda pops in his dark apartment were far better than being in the middle of a place like Bridgewater, but the tip on the graverobber left him intrigued and Dorse would be pleased with his find. Yes, on every other Thursday night of the year, he would be cozy at home thumbing through his scrapbook, catching up on late night television, and petting on Myra – the least complicated female he ever knew. She was fuzzy and feline. A Siamese cat picked up off the street one night after a standoff with Dorse that almost cost his position at the *Statesman*.

The clack of the glass hitting the bartop startled him.

"Shall I close out your tab, buddy bear?" the bartender asked. "I don't think I want you loitering around. Your kind ain't never fit in well here."

"What's your deal, baldy? I'm not a freeloading type," Vic muttered. He stared up at the man for a moment, maintaining a blank expression. "I'll keep the tab open. I'm in no rush."

"Fine... Have a Flitz on the house." He slammed the bottle on the bartop as it spewed foam down the sides.

Maybe I will write a hit piece on this dump.

"Watch yourself," Vic said, his voice remaining calm and collected. "I'm with the media... *man*. I could ruin you. The unemployment line gets awfully long this time of year for chumps like you."

The bartender walked away, shaking his head in apparent frustration.

The television above the bar played lousy and loud as Peter Jennings rambled about lingering devastation in the Middle East from Desert Storm. The cool burn of the "Ramsey Special" — three ounces of cola on top of two ounces of *Old Tymer's* took him to another place.

A man in a black t-shirt sat to his right, two or three days unshaven, and reeking of alcohol. His gravelly voice chirped, "How are you?"

"I'm good enough," Vic said.

"Your mind already wanderin' to la-la land after a few swigs of piss water?"

"I'm not much for small talk," Vic said, sipping on his cocktail.

"Me neither." The man rubbed his scruffy chin. "Yet, here we are. Two guys sittin' by each other in a bar with nothin' better to do than yammer the night away."

He extended his hand toward Vic. "Bob James. You can call me Livewire."

"Bob James? Could your parents come up with a sorrier name? Makes me think of a pointless B-Movie filler character."

Livewire laughed. "Probably... my parents were native to the region and adopted a European last name to help us fit in."

Vic picked up his Flitz, raising it toward Livewire, "Native, huh? My mother had that in her, too. Here, here." Clacking the bottles together, they both sipped on the Flitz.

I'm ready to gag on this crap.

"Piss water is the right name for it," Vic said, choked up from the burning aftertaste.

Livewire grinned at him as he swirled what was left in the bottle around. "Yeah, it's cheap, but, it works... I saw your badge. Your credentials, I mean. What are ya? You a reporter?"

Vic nodded. "That's right. Vic Ramsey, writer... shooter of the breeze... accentuated exaggerator... purveyor of platonic placation."

"Say what? You're talkin' too fast, word slinger."

"I'm a columnist. I work for the *Statesman*."

"I never cared for their drivel. Might as well be the Riverton Anvil as far as I'm concerned."

Vic chuckled. "I've thought the same thing... but it pays better than the unemployment line or the penny and nickel royalties I get from selling manuscripts."

"Here, here. I'll drink to that," Livewire said, finishing his Flitz and clanking it again with Vic's. "You still got a lot left... What's your next piece about?"

"That old hotel down the block."

Livewire gulped. "You mean... The Oak Hollow Hotel?"

Vid nodded. "Yeah, that's the one."

Livewire trembled as he worked to regain composure. "I'm not much for that place anymore. It ain't never been the same."

"The same since what...?"

"I'm sure you must remember hearin' about the fire."

"I've been back in town a couple of years," Vic said, hesitating, his eyes looking away a moment. "As far as news and media, I only work for them. I prefer to live under my rock and only come out when I have to."

Livewire moved closer to Vic, wrapping his arm around him and breathing in his face as several onlookers studied his growing inebriation. His voice grew loud, "Yep. The check in for guys like you at The Oak Hollow Hotel's a doozy, but that checkout can be a real bitch!"

"What are you saying?" Vic asked.

"I talked to that friend of yours..."

"What friend?" Vic asked, narrowing his eyes.

"You know... the swingin' fellow... he sat right there in the exact same seat as you." Livewire scratched the top of his head. "Guy was drinkin' some second-rate cocktail about like whatever the crap is you've got now. I came over and talked to him for a minute. I'll tell you one thing, he didn't seem right in the head, anymore."

"Are you a shrink? What makes you say that? I mean, he was always pretty straight-laced as far as the two of us were concerned."

"No. I'm not. That hotel warped him and it ruined him," Livewire said. "I did my best to set him straight. He'd been stayin' at the hotel for a while, right? How else can I say it? Extended stays never work out well there."

Vic studied the glass rings on the bartop. "I didn't realize his fate was common knowledge."

"Yeah... Oak Hollow's always had problems. No more of this mystical mumbo jumbo, though," Livewire said. "We speak too much of it and it'll follow us like a bad omen."

"Why do you say that?"

"I hear her voice..."

"Who?" Vic asked.

"I'm not going to say her name. She hears it when I call. I took it one step too far with her in '78, and she warped me. I remember it like it was yesterday. Our spirits have been intertwined in a way ever since.

I picked her up outside the school one day after class let out. We had dinner and drinks, a casual fling, nothing too fancy. Her teeth struck me as odd, bein' so chiseled and all, but as long as she didn't smile too big, it didn't bother me much. Once we closed down every joint in town, she brought me here to Oak Hollow. I'd heard stories from my mother about the Shaman disappearin' many years ago, and it grew to be an exaggerated folklore with time—not in the aging like a fine wine sort of way, but more like a bottle of Flitz after it's sat at room temperature for a week. Hah. We got over behind the old hotel building. I saw faces in the windows doin' God knows what with God knows who. She told me to focus on her and I did. She promised me she would show me things, tell me the meaning to my life... said she was psychic, you know, gifted with that sort of thing. She lit a campfire behind the building, tellin' me that was where she lived—that even though the place got a bad rap in the public eye, it offered great things. I was uncomfortable bein' so unchivalrous and watchin' her do all the work. The lady set the fire on her own, but her independence left a bigger impression on me. We sat there as the flames swayed back and forth, back and forth, and she sang and chanted the night away. I could have sworn she was an angel from heaven. It must have been well past midnight, and I was well past wasted. I started openin' up too much about my past... things I wish I could have seen and done. One thing led to another and I let it go too far. She promised me I would see granddad after our... ritual. I never saw him, but I felt him. Not in a good way, honestly. Memories triggerin' like they were my own, over and over at the worst of times and in the most vulnerable of situations. I'll tell you one thing, the second I stepped in or near that old hotel, he screamed so loud in my head I couldn't hear myself think. Just as soon as I convince myself I'm going looney, he stopped, and that's when I saw him lightin' the dynamite in my mind like I was right there, like it was my own memory. A sad ending. They never found the bodies."

I've got to go. This guy's got a bad mojo.

He chugged the rest of his Flitz, his face cringing from its cardboard infused flavoring. Then, he stood up, swilling his last gulp of the Ramsey Special to wash it down, and dropped a twenty on the counter.

"I'll be seein' you around," Livewire said.

Vic nodded. "Yeah. Dry yourself out a while, and we'll do this again real soon."

"You've got some Chipequa in you, too. Don't you?" Livewire asked.

"Yeah. Like I said before, on my mother's side."

Livewire nodded. "I could tell. Talk to you later."

I hope not. One conversation with you was one too many.

CHAPTER TEN

The bar closed and VIC RAMSEY's glowing Casio flashed 2:05. Driving toward his stake out point, he parked a block away from the cemetery. A quick study across the field of headstones yielded no figures, only the shadows of trees, and the chirp of the crickets calling into the nighttime sky. He penned some notes for his next piece.

It's an unappreciated job with minimal benefits. This, I must say. I wonder what career path leads a man to dig graves. A poor education? A fixation with the dead or the undead? Or, a shady, long-running family business? It's not unadmirable. Someone has to do it. I'm okay with the cremation myself, but to each his own. When my day of reckoning comes, he'll treat me just the same as all the rest, dropping dirt on me with his crummy, rusty shovel. No longer a person — just a mere statistic in a plot of 6x3 holes, due west of Clairmont Lane.
- VR

He rolled up the window to the Impala, locking the door as he climbed out, shutting it quietly until it clicked. Walking across the field of slabs somewhat methodically, he used various trees for cover, staking out a spot in the southeastern corner behind an old oak.

An hour went by and nothing notable had occurred. He drifted to sleep, catching his head as it drooped near the closest grave. The lone highlight of the hour was a squirrel that leapt from a tree to the top of a partially smashed headstone across from where he sat.

I guess I'll move somewhere else. This place is pretty spread out, anyhow.

He went across the cemetery, walking sloppier than when he began.

His mind wandered in the silence.

I'm glad I convinced that baldo to hand over an Old Tymer's to help the night go by. That was a good idea, after all. It's like fishing or deer hunting. You've just got to wait till they make an appearance. What am I, really? A phony drunk sitting next to a headstone. I better write that down. Shee-yit, you are living on the edge. Aren't ya, boy?

"It's time I start to blend in," he muttered aloud, tearing up his shirt, rubbing dirt on the sides of his face to better look the part, and mumbling a pile of garden variety obscenities to the sky above. As could be expected, the cemetery remained empty. The fog in the air left visibility a struggle.

He swigged another chug of the clear liquor.

I'll sit out for an hour and if they never show, I'll go on home.

The overnight air remained warm while he propped his head against the back of the headstone. It buckled, but he paid no mind.

It's no hotel pillow, but it'll do.

Singing to himself the lone song his father taught him as a child, Vic found solace in his drunken stuper. "O... The farmer in the dell... the farmer in the dell... hi ho... the dairy o..."

A flashlight shined toward him, interrupting his moment of jovial inebriation.

"What are you doing out there?" a woman's voice called out. She clicked the light off and on in a morse code like fashion. "This isn't a place to be after hours. Public intoxication is a crime, you know?"

"What's it to you?" he muttered in a slur, struggling to stand up. "You law enforcement?"

"No." She moved in closer toward him. "Just a concerned citizen." She clicked the flashlight off.

"Leave me be. I'm waiting for someone."

"And, who pray-tell, might that be?" her eyes glowing yellow, the silhouette of the moon shining behind her — her gray smock unflattering to her attractive figure.

"I don't know," he mumbled before stretching.

She walked over behind one of the graves next to an oak tree and pulled out a shovel. "Well, get to work and start digging. That way I don't have to boil up your innards and curse you like my gosh darn ex." She handed the shovel to him. "Over there... I need more of that sunbaked color."

"Color? I'm sure it's just a box of bones by now. What's it to you?"

"Are you an expert on the dead?" she asked. "Shut your dinky mouth before I make you choke on a piece of bark!"

"Sheesh, lady. Cut me a br...eak. I'm... pretty well wasted."

She studied him. "I hired you for a job, didn't I?"

Should I lie? Come on. Live on the edge, Ramsey.

"You sure did." He reached in his pocket, pulling out his notepad. "I have my note from the phone call the other day. I'm sorry. I got tired of waiting and one thing led to another with the booze. Forgive me."

"That's better. Get that lying out of your system, now." She grinned up at the nighttime sky. Her teeth were filed to sharp points — her wiry hair, an unaging charcoal. "It's forgivable. I'm not one for keeping tabs on unpardonable sins. That's between you and your maker."

Vic started pummeling the earth with the shovel.

Yep, this is going to take a while.

"You've got an hour. The moon's pretty tonight, isn't it? Dig faster. Don't worry... you won't hit any water or gas lines over here. Get aggressive with it."

Vic's heart pumped vigorously as he fought the urge to keel over. He stopped digging as the woman glared toward him.

Looking back into her eyes, he said, "I should have taken my nitro..."

"What?"

"My heart..." He yanked the pill bottle from his pocket, unscrewed the lid, and inhaled one. "It doesn't have much gas left in the tank. Doc says it's genetic. I've got a worsening case of angina. I'm overdue for a bypass. I'm just too anxious a guy to go under the knife."

"What a puny man. Taking middle of the night, grave robbing jobs with a heart problem? Are you an adrenaline junkie or do you just have a death wish? I know a guy in Michigan that can help keep you comfortable while he kills you if that's what you want. No man should go out laboring."

Vic looked toward her, breathless and out of words.

She laughed. "I see you need a jolt of some extra testosterone in your life — a spring in your step. You don't have a little woman to keep you in order? You know... someone to boss you around and keep you tidied up at home. Do you?"

"I don't."

"I'm sorry... maybe you're a nineties man?" She smiled at him. "We don't judge."

"No. I live alone."

"Well, I'm about to make your life a lot more interesting... a gal's got to get her needs met, too, you know?"

He fell to the ground as his body grew faint and the woman moved toward him, wrapping her arms around in a tight embrace.

CHAPTER ELEVEN

The overnight clerk position annoyed NANCY HELBENS, but it paid the bills. On busy weekends, a slew of guests would arrive in a rush when a neighboring convention or conference came to town or if Old Town Riverton had a guitar picker in the square worthy enough to gain the attention of those too wasted to head home.

As she understood it through the *Statesman's* long running story from the late Jake Calhoun, the hotel's unexpected restoration came about because of government grants, real-estate developer investments, and dated property deeds discovered in the hotel basement shortly after its near damning blaze nearly eight years earlier. She knew the backstory well, walking through the lobby on the quiet nights and reading over each of them with care. The walls in the northwest corner were covered in framed photographs and newspaper clippings recovered from the original hotel, chronicling its inception in 1926 and the restoration process that re-imagined the hotel as a boutique-styled outfit.

She had driven by the place once or twice before getting the position, but avoided the area, given her previous struggles. It was strange, sitting behind a desk in almost the same spot she once worked before. There was zero resemblance to Creepy Nights or its short-lived glory days at 5454 Oak Hollow Lane.

The golden pendulum on the antiquated Seth Thomas neared its final moment of ascension until it's plummet into the next half hour. She tidied the pens, the sticky notes, and the brochures and pamphlets that graced the desktop and yawned.

I don't think I can stay awake much longer...

The surrounding room was bright, colorful, and wide open, with additional tapestries, gaming tables, and well positioned taxidermy, easily the finest handiwork of its kind in all of Riverton. The CRT monitor and matching keyboard and mouse on her desk were a yellowing taupe. After a quick perusal of the area for unseen visitors, she lit up a cigarette, ducking under the desk a moment to puff out the smoke. She laid the cancer stick on top of the mainframe beneath to keep it contained.

Dropping her head on the lobby counter, she searched her mind thinking on the separation from Ron, and of Randy, still optimistic of his return.

Randy, I miss you, son.

***

She awoke the next morning, having forgotten that she had laid a piece of pink chewing gum on the desk. It was tangled in her hair.

She cursed. *What did I miss?*

She tried to separate her hair from the gum but it wasn't happening. Without a blunt, edgier cut, she would have no choice but a lopsided mess trying to tend to it herself.

The basement barber — I guess he can do women's hair, too... Business is slow enough. I bet I can sneak down there.

Entering the basement, she noted Greenwich absent from his office. She tiptoed in, flipping through his day planner. It was empty. Not a single appointment or meeting booked. Nancy wandered out into the basement common area as the barbershop pole caught her attention.

The blue and red on white spinning. Spinning, spinning, spinning. So pretty.

She approached the check-in desk to speak, but her voice was absent.

The oddball barber stood in front of her, staring — one eye closer to the nose than the other. He looked distressed. Despite no other customers, he delayed. A blunt cut was not in her plan at the start of the day.

"It'll be a few minutes," he said. "Have a seat."

His imperfections remind me of mine. I might even make a friend. Who knows?

She sat on the bench, expecting the wood to give beneath her shapely endowments. The barber shop pole lulled her. Drifting away, little by little, she softly snored.

The cock-eyed barber squalled toward her and she awoke.

"Take a seat, my dear lady. I've got some fashion mags if that suits your fancy, or if you're more of an outdoorsy type, there's a *Hunter's Digest* I can dig out."

"No thanks," she said.

"Suit yourself. I thought I remembered you reading before."

"Before? I've been working at the hotel for over a month... I'm surprised I haven't run into you before now."

"Yeah, you're on night shift usually, right? This barber works banker's hours... nine to two, with a two-hour lunch. Greenwich has those cameras... I sit in there and watch the lobby cameras when I'm bored."

Weirdo.

He pulled out the scissors, motioning toward her hair. "What'll it be?" he asked.

Something's off about this.

"Six inches on the sides. An inch off the bangs."

"Okay. Do we need to touch up any roots yet? I see gray coming in."

The radio cued a *Tom Petty* song — a wobbling voice with dreamy acoustic guitars. He dropped the scissors and pulled out a straight-edged razor, cutting inches of her hair off, progressively getting more aggressive with the blade. Nancy's hair flew across the room as he sliced and diced.

Looking in the mirror just ahead, she struggled to see herself. She could only focus on the crosshatched horizontal red stripes on his shirt, reminding her of the menacing character from *Freaky Fred*.

He grumbled as he trimmed, "I know your type."

"My type? I said six inches."

He started swiping toward her neck with the blade like he was trying to nick her, but there was no blood.

"You feel that? Can you feel it?" he yelled.

He lunged toward her full force with the blade poking through the back of the barber chair just to the right of her body.

"What's going on?" she groaned. "What are you doing?"

"Get out of the chair, now," he retorted.

She gritted her teeth. "Excuse me? I'll pay you for the cut. Just get on with it."

The barber's BO permeated the room. She struggled to breathe as his sweat dripped to the floor and the room steamed up. Her eyes locked onto the fogging mirror as flames danced behind her. Whirling around to inspect the area, she realized there was no fire.

What's going on?

Losing all control of herself, she said, "Go ahead. Just kill me."

No. No. That's not me. I'm not saying that.

She interrupted her racing thoughts, "Hey... Hey... I'm sorry. That's not my way to say something like that. Please, finish my haircut."

He brought the trim to a close, showing Nancy the finished product in the mirror.

"It's fine. Thanks."

"Now, get on," he said. "I don't want any trouble."

"I'm not the enemy here. What's your problem?"

"This conversation is over," he grumbled. "Get out before Greenwich busts you for leaving the front desk unmanned."

She awoke, sitting on the bench. The barber was busy with another guest. Her hair was shorter. She remained unsure how she ended up asleep in the chair.

Time for me to get out of here. She waved at the barber. He grinned back, flicking the straight bladed razor into the air and mimicking a throat slitting motion.

CHAPTER TWELVE

Waking in a dark room, the lingering scent of the woman remained all over VIC RAMSEY.

What did that aggressive hag do to me?

He fumbled his way through the space until arriving at a spring with a trickling waterfall. There were only faint lights on the ceiling. Six canvases stood on easels, surrounding the spring full of water. He could make out flesh toned figures, but the faces were faded and washed out. Studying the area for the woman, he convinced himself he was alone. He climbed in, dipping his body into the spring to get rid of the lingering scent. It helped. The alcohol previously consumed left him desperate for water. He cupped his hands, sipping on the sustenance offered from the spring. The woman emerged from beneath it. Her face more youthful, her body more chiseled than he recalled.

"I was wondering when you might come in for a dip," she said, studying him closely. "After last night, you needed one. Ha-ha."

Vic's heart pounded in a merciless repetition. "What do you mean?"

Her voice became authoritative. "Drink up. Let's get that heart under control. I know you haven't laid eyes on a woman that way since Watergate. Or was it... when Sputnik was launched? I'm sorry. I don't mean to make light of your... shortfalls."

"I'm the one with the problem. Where are we?"

"What did you think, though?" she asked. "You more alive, yet?"

"I don't remember a thing."

"Fair enough," she tucked her hair back, wrapping it in a scrunchy as she dressed in a gray smock. "It does wonders for the figure, doesn't it?"

"I'm not going to lie to you," he said, splashing water from the spring onto himself. "Your figure is just fine. That smock is not."

She grinned. "That's all part of the game. Thanks for passing the test. There's no room for a lying tongue around here. Never has been."

He studied her face a moment. There was something familiar about it, but he couldn't place it.

"Sit on that stone," she said. "I've got to finish you."

"Excuse me?" he asked.

"The painting... I've got to finish your silhouette. I hope I didn't sketch you too stumpy. Underneath those baggy hand-me-downs your wearing is a nicely fit man for your age."

He blushed, a forward woman like this, an artist, might be exactly what was missing from his life.

"Where the hell am I?" he asked.

"It's a fair question, but last night you told me you liked a good mystery. Why would I want to solve the riddle so quickly? Sip on some more from the spring." She leaned in closer to him, "it'll keep you young if you treat it right."

He moved toward her, resting his hand on her shoulder, feeling as if something other than himself had control.

Something's gone wrong, he thought. *What was in that drink?*

The woman crumbled away to the floor, and it bottomed out under her. Her screams and cackles echoing loudly as she formed again, stretching her hands out and across Vic's body and pulling him further and further into an unending abyss. There were chilling voices, yelling, desperately longing for relief, and yet, there was nothing he could do as he plummeted into a momentary hell. There it was, right in front of him, the night of the accident — the same one that killed his parents. The crash was vivid.

What were the odds of a drunken head on collision with your own family? One in a million? One in a billion?

Somehow, Vic Ramsey was spared. He never deserved it. He ran as far as he could to escape until the unrelenting call of Riverton beckoned him home. He passed out on the floor as the woman hovered above.

***

He awoke feeling pain course through his body — the searing torture of the hot poker on his arm more than he could bear as he screamed to the sky. Agatha carried him across the tunnel. Bound and gagged, she shoved him toward the glowing fire as it burned, flicking paint on him.

"This won't be too bad for you, Victor. You have a thing for heat. I guess I shouldn't admit this, but I've watched you for a while, honey. I get bored sometimes. Your pathetic habits aren't anything interesting."

I've got to get out of here, now, he thought. *Live on the edge for a single night and I end up stuck in a nightmare with the damn devil's wife.*

"I fired us up some soup and sandwiches," she said, putting them on a primitive hotplate. "What do you say?"

Vic's voice remained muffled as he attempted a reply.

"Oh, I'm sorry." She giggled toward him, speaking to someone around the corner in a lighter tone. "How about I have one and you two can just stay put?"

Vic's brow furrowed as a soft whistle echoed across.

Who else is in here?

"Mmm... that's good," she said. "Grilled cheese and tomato soup. Perfect combination for an old broad. Warms up the heart, doesn't it?"

Old broad? You look pretty young to me.

She finished the sandwich and walked out of the room.

"I'll see you in a while. I've got to get to work. These paintings won't sell themselves and I don't reckon 'ol Honest Steve will buy from me again anytime soon. I burned that bridge."

CHAPTER THIRTEEN

NANCY HELBENS' reluctance to meet with Ron was superseded by business — neither of them being thrilled to meet in person after Randy's disappearance. Whether it was to bury the hard feelings for the decision to lie low about it or a mutual frustration about the separation was unclear. They grabbed a coffee across town at the Perk-a-Lator coffee shop, a shabby-chic joint that drew the yuppies of Riverton with great regularity at all hours of the day. The exposed brick wall in the room and the guitar picker's corner typically featured mediocre musicians taking a stab at their favorite covers or their own forgettable originals. This afternoon in particular, Nancy and Ron fared fortunately as the stage remained empty while they sipped their coffee, and a neighboring speaker offered a ghost loving number from *Crash Test Dummies*.

"So, how's work?" Ron asked, looking away from her, clearly uncomfortable with meeting up in public.

"It's a job. What about you? Got anything promising lined up?"

"Funny you should ask. I just took an abstract balloon artist position at the nervous hospital... I'll start later this week."

She grinned. "Really, Ron? I've never seen you as that kind of caring type. The good news is," she reached across to pat him on the shoulder. Her voice dropped to a whisper, "I picture you fitting in just fine with the residents. Maybe the doctors will admit you too after they study you a while."

"Gee, thanks."

"That was free," she said, sipping on her coffee. "I'm thinking about a career in dry-witted and cynical comedy."

His eyebrows raised. "Are you serious?"

"No, Ron. The real reason we're here... Why don't you tell me why you locked yourself in a lease without consulting me? That's kind of ridiculous. I've got two proposals."

He crossed his arms. "Okay. Go ahead, then."

"Option one, we sell the house. You stay in your apartment, I'll live in the hotel, and we split the proceeds of the sale and go our separate ways..."

"Or?"

"Or, we forfeit the lease on your apartment, you live in the house that's already been paid for, and I'll just stay at the hotel. I know which option I'm leaning towards."

Ron looked at his watch and sipped on his coffee. "This is too cold. Ugh. What are you leaning towards?"

"I don't want to sway the jury. You're a grown man. You speak *your* choice and the reasoning behind it, and we'll either argue our way into an agreement or have us a stack of divorce papers finalized. I just... I'm not sure what's best for Randy right now."

"Does it matter?" he whispered, his face weepy. "Do you think we're actually going to find him?"

"I haven't given up yet." She stood up. "I'll be right back. You need a warm up?"

"Sure. It's an Americano."

"Walk over with me? Just be smart enough to talk in code."

"Nancy, I know..."

They approached the coffee bar as Nancy reordered their second round.

This'll keep me up all night. I guess that's a good thing for this job.

"I think the key thing here, Nancy, is that we need to figure out if our future is going to be patched up or separated. I know I have little to offer right now. I've just been in a rut for a while. If I'm honest, I'm thinking about getting back into radio. I know it's in the public eye, but I feel like that spark inside me is coming back for the first time in years."

"Is the balloon artist gig going to afford you the apartment in the meantime?" she asked.

"I qualified for the government assistance. I don't need to make much. That's the best way to milk the system. As much as I don't trust them, I might as well stick it to 'em until they hunt me down in the middle of the night and slit my throat."

She shook her head. "I didn't think so."

The coffee guy looked up at Nancy and made eye contact.

She studied Ron's eyes. "Why are you so scared? You selling military secrets to the Soviets or what?"

"They have black ops. That's a real thing."

"I like your *big...* imagination, Ron," she said, looking toward the coffee guy and widening her eyes. "It keeps me intrigued."

"I say we sell the house and split the proceeds."

They carried their next cup of coffee back to the table.

"If we ever decide to hook up our bumpers again and make this thing work, we can give a good down payment on something better," he said.

"I guess that settles it, then. I better get back to the hotel. My manager's a bit of a shoulder surfing greaseball."

"A what?" Ron replied, frustrated by Nancy's description of Greenwich.

She nodded. "He likes to stay in my hair and make sure I'm doing what he needs me to."

"What he needs you to? What does *that* include? Is he treating you okay?"

"He's fine. Don't get all protective. Five minutes ago, you could barely stomach looking at me. Now, you're wanting to get that way? I'm okay with admitting we're estranged, Ron. It's not a secret."

They walked into the parking lot. Ron leaned toward Nancy and tried to hug her straight on as they stood outside. She pulled away, instead giving him a side hug.

"Call me if you hear anything about Randy," she said.

"Likewise." He started to walk away from the lot.

"Where's the car?" she called out.

"I didn't bring it, Nancy. I'm headed to the bus stop."

"I don't get your disjointed distrust for the government. It's irrational. Every damn thing is a conspiracy and yet you trust municipal transportation managed by local government like that's the best way to get yourself from point A to point B?"

"That's my business," he said. "See you later. Good luck with your shift tonight. Don't let the greaseball hover too close. You don't want to end up with another kid, do you?"

She rolled her eyes, moving toward their burgundy Caprice wagon. "Goodnight."

CHAPTER FOURTEEN

VIC RAMSEY awoke in a dark room. Studying each of its walls, he noted bones of varying sizes, ages, and qualities stacked on shelves — stark indicators of a peculiar purpose. Vats of bone paste lined the walls, as did varying canvases that were mounted all around. Each of them was clearly symbolic of a greater meaning and purpose, but nonetheless beyond Vic's level of comprehension. Candlelight surrounded him as he reclined on a bed of feathers. He was no longer bound and gagged. Instead, he laid in a posh robe, with a decadent tray of cheeses and fruits placed in front of him.

The woman's voice carried from the next room. She spoke softer and sweeter, "What business did you have moseying your way around out there, anyhow? I know you would never lie to me. Momma doesn't like it when you lie."

The glow of a fire shined through the empty keyhole on the other side of the door. Vic climbed out of the makeshift bed, opting to observe the woman through the small opening. As he studied the area closer, the woman's voice spoke with authority. "You're a very special boy," she said, ruffling the red hair on top of the child's head, "I want you to know that. Sip on some of momma's soup."

"You're not my..." the boy called out.

She came closer toward him, shoving her finger in front of his lips. "Shut up. Your time's almost up with me."

"I'm sorry," he said, his voice dejected. He pulled away, sitting down on a stone that doubled as a chair.

"Sorry doesn't cut it anymore. You are going to honor your mother, and that's final. You refuse to do that and daddy won't have his tongue anymore, will he? We'll filet it on the fire and have us a feast. What do you think?"

Who do you have in there? he thought. *That poor kid.*

As he peeked through the narrow keyhole toward the child, he noted the unspeakable terror showing through the boy's eyes as the woman moved close toward him, crowding his space as she stroked a paintbrush down the side of his cheek. Crimson droplets dripped to the floor.

"Is that bl...?"

She cupped her hand over his mouth. "Shut up, boy... Hey, what's that?" she asked, moving toward the door that Vic stood behind.

He swiftly moved toward the bed, situating himself to look as if he were still asleep as she had earlier positioned him.

She stood up on top of a large stone. "There's a roach over there. You know how much I hate them. Kill it now!"

The footsteps neared until there was a pounding sound.

"Stomp it! Stomp it!" she said. "It's on the floor."

POUND! POUND!

"I can't handle it. It makes my skin crawl. You awake in there, Victor?" she asked from the other side of the door.

Vic struggled to utter a word, instead grunting.

"Good. I'll see you in a minute, joy boy."

***

He sat on the feathered bed as Agatha entered the room. Her hair was tucked back in a tight bun, the gray smock still wrapped around her body.

You look older, he thought.

She pulled out an antiquated metronome from a closed off area.

"Well, my friend," she said, wrapping her arm around his shoulder, "I suppose it's about time we uh... get better acquainted again, isn't it? I'll set the tempo."

"Better acquainted? What are you talking about?"

"We've got to unpack the past to get you back in the present. Your memories might as well be on life support. Don't you remember your crazy life in New Orleans? I took you and your friend there before..."

"I've never been to New Orleans... I spent a few years in Des Moines. Never New Orleans."

"Oh, honey... how quickly the warped mind crumbles away. I'll set you straight."

His eyes drooped as she lit incense. "This ought to loosen you up." The metronome grew louder as she continued speaking to him. "Close your eyes and keep lying down. You need a reminder. It will take a bit to dig around to get to the right spot."

The metronome was in motion.

CLICK. CLACK. CLICK. CLACK.

"A few moons ago, you were fooling around in the French Quarter. Drinking... having a good time... and then BAM! Out of nowhere, you're collapsed in the middle of Bourbon Street and convulsing like you're cursed. You grab at your chest like you've been violated. Looking into the sky, you see an old lady poking a voodoo doll in one of the upstairs rooms just above. Everyone else around is paying no mind to you. Partying. Flashing tatas — the whole nine yards. The old broad stares at you stabbing that little doll over and over like she had a bone to pick with you. You're too snowblind to fathom anymore — up until a good Samaritan takes you to the nearest hospital. Eventually, you fumble your way out of town, one bender after the next, until you make your way back to Riverton. You short-circuited your brain one time too many in your earlier days. Didn't you, Victor? There's not a day you don't regret it. I pulled you out of your struggle. I saw you hobbling down the block, struggling to walk a straight line. That awful blue sweatshirt. I took you in and I sheltered you. Don't you remember? Herbal remedies, chants and incantations, tree hugging, smoking... toking."

CLICK. CLACK. CLICK. CLACK.

"I'm going to stop the metronome, now. Think long and hard. Come back to mommy."

He spoke under his breath slowly while hypnotized, "Agatha... it's you. You picked me up from a million shattered pieces and put me back together one by one. Only the love a mother could have."

She fell back in her chair in a momentary ecstasy, swallowing the flattering comments, despite her deceit. As she stopped the metronome, he awoke, studying her eyes.

"You saw yourself through that keyhole, didn't you?" she asked. "I was there with you, Vic. I've been a part of you longer than you can remember... my lost and vulnerable puppy — desperate for shelter. You're safe with mommy. You always will be."

That's not what I remember. You're trying to delude me, he thought.

She turned up *Creedence Clearwater Revival,* dancing in circles around him.

His mind remained stuck on a loop as he drifted to sleep, the same lulling song playing as the flames swayed back and forth. His mantra flashed in bright white incandescently lit letters on top of a black sky that slid up and down the walls as they caved in around him.

It's a beautiful time to unwind... it's a beautiful time to unwind... it's a beautiful time to...

WAKE UP!

He awoke in the middle of the cemetery in one of the dug-up plots, staring at the clouds as they ran across the front of the moon. He remained unclear on what experiences were his own, someone else's, or a muddy mess of the past and present waging an unbeatable war against one another.

Following leads has gotten me into trouble before, but never quite this way.

CHAPTER FIFTEEN

NANCY HELBENS studied the night sky behind the Oak Hollow Hotel as she took a drag. The shift from Lucky Strike to Marlboro seemed a natural one; though the aftertaste was indeed different (Though, Greenwich might have debated her on this). Most nights, there were no other colleagues to chat with, so she often talked to the air or whatever bird or owl was in proximity. It never bothered her, though. Socializing was an opportunity, but never a necessity. Greenwich had given her a chance at the last place she would have imagined returning, and the pay was better, too.

The cops in the area no longer took her seriously as her stories of captivity grew bigger, brighter, and more colorful with time. Her well-seasoned flavor of life in the tunnel had grown extravagant, as did the evolving description of her captor. She briefly capitalized on the lingering fanfare, landing interviews on the local news, *NightWatch*, and a feature article in the *Statesman* a few years earlier.

Popping the back door of the hotel open, she entered the lobby. The lights flickered and flashed. There were shadows and silhouettes across various corners of the room. Nancy rubbed her eyes.

It's the chronic insomnia. I can't seem to adjust to sleeping during the morning hours when the sun's up. Momma just needs more rest...

A woman's voice called from the basement, "You leave your post unmanned for a while... and strange things happen. Don't they, Nancy? Don't be so sloppy, child."

Nancy approached the room, ensuring her footing didn't clomp across the floor. Her heart pounded through her neck.

No... no... not happening again...

A canvas stood on an easel on the far side. As Nancy drew nearer, a swooping pallet of matching flesh-toned colors stood before her. It had a distinct and unsettling odor.

I'm going to gag. Ugh.

She walked around the back of the easel and found a yellow sticky note attached with a crimson red lipstick kiss mark.

Nancy,

It's been a pleasure

Sincerely,

You know who

P.S. I left the little red-head on your mommy's doorstep.

Not going to call her... Not going to call her now. I can't handle this.

She shoved the note in her pocket, moving across to the lobby desk and rifling through the hotel Rolodex in a panic.

Riverton PD Non-emergency line

She picked up the phone and dialed the number.

A voice came on the line, "Riverton PD. How can we help?"

"It's Nancy Helbens.... I'm at The Oak Hollow Hotel. I'm being harassed."

The voice mumbled something to some others in the background. The affect of being switched to a speakerphone caused her voice to echo through the line. "You know what our policies are for dealing with Precinct Three. Don't you, lady?"

She ran her fingers through her graying chestnut hair. "I'm well aware. Send someone right away, please."

"Alright. We'll get someone over soon."

A group of chuckles came through the phone.

Go ahead and laugh all you want.

She hung up. Looking around the lobby further for the harasser seemed pointless. She sat down at the desk, her breath remaining elevated. The stench of the canvas unsettled her as her mind went back to the last time she smelled burned flesh as a child.

Bobbie Helbens and her friend, Agatha Haney, giggled on the back patio as they leafed through culinary magazines. Nancy sat just inside the house with the television on but had her ear pressed up against the window's screen, occasionally peeking back at her mother.

"I think I'll make the jello mold next week," Agatha said. "How about you, honey?"

"I'm going to make a jellied-veal loaf. You think Mitch will like it?"

Agatha looked at Bobbie. "Oh, honey. He's going to love it. Bottom's up."

Bobbie grinned. They clanked their glasses together. "Mmm... mmm... mmm! That is a fine and fancy wine, my dear."

"You're always so sweet to me, Bobbie. I'm starting to think Nancy may be jealous of all the time we're logging."

Bobbie cackled into the air. "That old black and white television's one hell of a babysitter, isn't it?"

"Yes, but a good mother's got to invest quality time to make her child well. Too much neglect and she'll just explode at the worst possible times." Agatha sipped on her wine. "You can quote me on that."

Bobbie snapped, splashing wine into Agatha's face. "What the hell are you trying to get at, witch? Why are *you* commenting on how I should raise my kid? Don't tell another lady what to do. You shouldn't meddle in business that's not your own!"

"Good grief. Lighten up. I'm going to have to take you down the block for some shock therapy, honey. You're so tense," Agatha said, massaging Bobbie on the shoulder, remaining strangely relaxed.

Bobbie shook her head. "I'm sorry. I'm just... stressed. I shouldn't have done that."

"It's okay, honey. I've got a group I'm putting together that I think will be just the medicine from the earth you need."

She peered into Agatha's eyes. "Really? What kind of group?"

"Oh, it's just getting you more in touch with nature. Those inner parts of yourself that you suppress to keep peace with people. We have to let out the pinned-up rage sometimes. Life's too short to burn it all up in waves of fury."

"You have such a way with words," Bobbie said, looking at Agatha in admiration.

"I think we're both just tipsy. Ha-ha."

They looked at each other and laughed.

"Let's peel some bark off that live oak tree," Agatha said. "I have something I want to show you. It will open your mind."

"Oh, man. Mitch will kill me if I touch that thing. He treats it like it's his idol."

"I think it's about time we set that straight. You got a match for your cigarettes?"

"I do," Bobbie said, handing it over to Agatha.

Agatha approached the tree, tearing off a piece, lighting the match and catching the corner on fire. She came back to Bobbie, dragging the burning bark across the side of her arm.

"Oh, honey. That control... it scares all the bad away. All those voices and feelings inside you don't want to have. It's a rush. You want to try it?"

"No. I'd rather not."

Agatha leaned in toward her, jabbing the burning oak into the side of Bobbie's arm. "Yes, you do, honey. Free yourself from the shackles. You're not just a housewife or a mother. You're an unappreciated saint."

Bobbie shrieked, dropping to the ground in tears.

Agatha looked toward the window. "We have us a spy. How about I teach her to respect her mommy's privacy...?"

"Agatha, that's unnecessary. I'd like you to leave. We're drunk."

"Fine. Fine. I'm leaving. I'll call you when I get the group together."

Bobbie remained on the ground on her hands and knees, traumatized by Agatha's bizarre action. The bizarre bark burner passed through the house looking at Nancy. She clicked off the television and got in Nancy's face and whispered, "She's a terrible mom, Nancy. One day you'll wake up to this and ditch her like she deserves." Agatha jammed the burning piece of oak bark into the side of her own arm. "Ah, nice! Smell the burn, baby. Your... momma won't know what hit her."

***

Detective Neil Penske entered the lobby of The Oak Hollow Hotel as Nancy sat lost in thought. The starched white shirt and blue slacks he wore fit him well, a clear evidence of his recent promotion to senior detective.

"Helbens, I heard you're over here crying wolf and I thought I would try to squash this before it gets out of hand. How many hours of my department's time have you wasted sending us back into that tunnel through the years? Somehow, you end up working at this place again. Crazy thing! We gave up looking around because we could find nothing conclusive enough to corroborate the details. I caught glimpses of the madness with Herbert, God rest his soul, but it was never tangible enough for me to admit it into evidence. There are bigger fish to fry around here. You know that."

Nancy shook her head at Penske. "How can you say that? This place has a hold on you, too. I see it in your eyes."

He sighed, taking a seat on one of the rounded lobby benches, and motioning her to come and sit down. "I've already said this, but I feel I need to say it again to get through to you and get you past your delusions. We've heard your sad story all over the television with all the darn cameras in town and the interviews a few years ago. We all know *Wilkerson* was a creep that manipulated all of you in a twisted slew of mind games back in '83... That you worked in the building before. I still can't understand what would draw you back to working here, though. If you're burned that bad, I'd be the heck out of Dodge. It all just seems preposterous considering the extravagant yarns you've spun on the tube."

[Creeper Joe was purged from Nancy's memories while inside the hotel, her union with Level Zero — nothing more than a distant haze.]

"That's all in the past," she said flatly.

"It's okay to admit it. Wilkerson's as good as dead and buried."

"It's not that simple, Neil. How many chats do we have to have for you to grasp that I'm not just making this stuff up?" She pulled out a cigarette and lit it up. "I'll just catch the wrath for smoking inside when Greenwich wakes up in the morning. These damn city bans on smoking indoors are a royal pain. Do you mind? Please don't write me up." She took her first puff.

"I don't care. As for Wilkerson, he's well past dead. It's probably better for all of us that he's not taking up space in our city cemetery."

"You can't say that." She huffed smoke away from Penske. "We all remember when the body went missing. That made national headlines, and it's an odd phenomenon. Perfect for tabloid fodder in a sleepy town with forgotten secrets. Who steals a body from a funeral home?"

"He's been gone for years. I touched his cold dead hands myself before 'ol Abel took him down to Cedar City."

Penske pulled out a notepad, retrieving a pencil from a cup on the hotel desk. "Alright, I'm here. Why don't you talk me through what prompted you to call, then?"

"It's the canvas in the break room."

"Canvas? You got a nutty Jackson Pollock lover or something?"

She squinted her eyes. "Not funny."

Entering the room, the canvas was nowhere to be seen.

Nancy's face grew flushed. "It was right there. I swear. Look around. I'm sure we'll find it."

Penske laughed, turning around to exit the room. "Nancy, I'm not wasting another darn second with you. Life experience has taught me two important truths — avoid liars and timeshares."

Nancy kicked at the floor. "I swear I'm not lying to you. I have no reason to make this stuff up."

He patted her on the shoulder. "That's okay, Nancy. I know you're... different. It's forgivable. I won't fine you for the emergency services dispatch call. We've always turned a blind eye to Precinct Three. It's easier that way..."

"I called the non-emergency number, anyway! Everyone says that about the blind eye... but nobody explains why..."

As Penske turned away, Nancy mimicked a strangling motion toward him.

Useless. That's the last time I'll call you jokers. Maybe Ron's right. You've all been bought off.

Penske exited the hotel.

***

Nancy phoned Ron from the hotel lobby.

"Hello?" he answered, half asleep.

"Ron, I'm sorry to call so late. You won't believe this..."

"Believe what?"

"I just received a tip on Randy. I got a note saying they dropped the kid off at mom's house. Can you go get him? I'll come by the apartment tomorrow."

Excitement rushed through his voice, "Oh my gosh. Thank God! That's great news. I'll hop on the bus and be there in a jiffy."

Nancy gawked. "A jiffy? Tch. Come on, Ron! Drive the Daihatsu and get him, stat. I don't want him riding on some dirty old bus. I can't afford to leave my shift this soon. Go pick him up, and I'll swing by your apartment tomorrow after I sleep off my shift. Make sure mom didn't overdo it with the pampering or whatever the hell else she does when she has too much free time with him."

"Nancy, I've got this under control. I'll get him."

She hung up the phone, studying the clock on the back wall.

Time to put up the 'Ring Bell for Service' placard and take a rest.

She followed the steps into the basement. The area was mostly dark. There was only the glow of the barbershop pole and a purple toned INFORMATION CENTER sign that flashed. It was misplaced compared to the rest of the hotel's theme and it bothered Nancy, but Greenwich insisted he like the charm and the white noise its buzz offered while on. She passed on through, settling into her private room, opting to remain in her mahogany red hotel uniform in case of overnight calls from the five or six customers checked into the hotel. She sat in the easy chair and popped it out.

Friggin' plaid print everywhere. God help us all.

John Grisham's wordsmithing lulled her to sleep as she cozied up. The bulb in the lamp next to her chair burned out.

***

POUND. POUND. POUND.

Getting up groggily from the chair, she approached the peephole. Jerry Greenwich stood outside the room, placing his eye up close to it to peer through.

I bet you wish it was reversed, creep. Back off, and I'll give you something to cry about, she thought.

Stepping back after knocking, his frustrated look lingered as he swooped the singular strands of hair across the top of his bald head.

POUND. POUND. POUND.

"Helbens, why aren't you manning the desk?" he grumbled, taking a moment to scratch his butt. His wife beater and polka dotted boxer shorts left little to her imagination.

He's probably hoping I'd return the favor and be that casual in my evening outfits with him. We're not roommates, dummy...

She yelled through the door, "You told me, you were okay with the on-call. It was 3AM, and I put the placard up like usual. Is there a problem with that?"

His voice elevated, "Watch yourself... I got a complaint from a customer saying they phoned the front desk and no one answered. Don't let it happen again.

I don't want to get any three-star reviews. *Hotel Digest* will equate us with the damn La Quinta downtown, otherwise."

"I'm sorry, sir," she said. "I thought I had the telephone set to forward to my room."

"I got it taken care of for you. It is now."

Now, aren't you a sweetheart, Jerry? Leave me alone.

CHAPTER SIXTEEN

An energetic drive into the neighborhood kept VIC RAMSEY bouncing as *Snap!* played through his speakers with the windows down. He tapped his hand on the dash in beat with the music as it blared. Neighbors washed their cars, mowed their grass, and children rode their bicycles down the symmetrical street — a picture perfect view of southern Americana at its finest.

This is great. Driving buzzed with a revoked license for years and not stopped a single time. Murphy's Law is bound to catch up with me one of these days.

Pulling into his driveway, he studied his home with pride. A visible evidence of his escape from the dirt floor he was born into, despite his parents' efforts to overcome it. There simply wasn't enough money in cotton to sustain them all through his childhood.

I'll never be impoverished like that again.

He reminded himself of this daily. His two-story lot and block home carried the most vanilla of features — nothing more than a pile of home improvement store supplies piecemealed in sixty days like clockwork. It matched the other three-hundred homes just like it up and down the street. It was more than sufficient. He went inside the house, shucking off his green necktie, kicking his shoes into the hall closet, and drifting to the refrigerator for a can of orange soda pop and a bag of pretzel rods.

He pulled out the family photo album – a miserable memento of his early years and nine monochrome photos commemorating his troubled childhood. Looking them over each night, he began his nightly unwinding rituals. His mother's eyes were as dark as her hair, her skin as olive as the loveliest of ladies he could recall. Their two photos together sat side by side, one at a farewell ceremony for his grandmother, and the other leaning against the sheets of scrap metal his parents called a home. The other photographs were simpler and non-descriptive to specific events. The shot was likely snapped by one of the richer relatives on his father's side coming to visit from the north during the winter season — always a witness to the poverty, but never concerned enough to offer them a path to a better life, despite their considerable wealth.

As for Vic, he remained a bachelor — rarely interested in anything more than pleasantries with a waitress or co-worker. Loneliness was not something to achieve — it was a way of life he came to embrace. The simplicity and freedom it offered kept him contented. There was one common theme in his home, and that was his scrapbook of pasted newspaper articles and photographs collected since arriving again in Riverton. Each night he looked over the contents with his magnifying glass, perusing for new details, occasionally pulling out a highlighter or a black-inked Bic to mark something he considered notable. The hobby was a private affair. He tucked it beneath the couch cushion as he tired, stretching out on the forest green sofa, repeating his evening mantra, "it's a beautiful time to unwind... it's a beautiful time to unwind... it's a beautiful time to..."

Myra hopped onto his lap and was already snoozing, her soft purr a reminder of her trust in her introverted owner. Vic drifted as the hum of the television faded away.

Only a few minutes later, the telephone rang.

"Ramsey, it's Dorse. I just wanted to check in and see how the write-up on the old hotel was coming along. I've signed off on the articles for some of the others around town, which I've enjoyed, but The Oak Hollow Hotel is the one I'm after and we both know that. You've told me for months you were going to start on it and all I see is you putting it off and going everywhere but there. I like what you've been doing and everything, but Oak Hollow is a great way to beef up the content in miscellaneous metro. I tried going over to the lobby to meet you the other day when you said you'd be checking in for a couple of days. The lady at reception told me you hadn't arrived or even made a reservation yet. Quit putting it off! We need to keep this piece alive. We're getting complaint letters and people are ready for the next installment."

"Probably because we never featured an article on Jake's swinging escapade earlier in the year," Vic said, looking down at his watch. "I'll check in sometime in the next day or two."

"Good enough. Speak to you soon."

The line disconnected.

Vic drifted back to sleep.

CHAPTER SEVENTEEN

It had been fifty-four days since Randy's disappearance (fifty-five counting the night he was dropped off). NANCY HELBENS arrived to pick him up from Ron's apartment. The shutters to the building were falling off as the puke green trim flecked off the edges. A woman leaned her head out the upstairs window with a spoon as she prepped for her next hit and watched a dealer loiter in a neighboring station wagon.

I guess this really is government assisted living. I don't want Randy staying here anymore.

It was only her second visit with Ron since the separation. Walking into the apartment without knocking, her eyes widened at the disorder.

What a piss poor example of a home. You are a winner, aren't you?

The room reeked of carelessness. Wadded up socks and laundry were piled up all over in no particular order. Garbage stood in piles, stacked on cabinets, tables, and in corners. Stale pizza boxes sat to the sides of the couch as flies buzzed around. Ron's feet were propped on the coffee table as he flicked through a guitar magazine and balanced a bottle of Flitz between his legs. Randy was mindlessly entertained by a Sega. A cassette tape blared *Primus* as Ron and Randy bobbed their heads.

D-I-V-O-R-C-E!

"What is this crap?" she yelled, picking up the band's *Frizzle Fry* cassette. "What's he saying? Too many puppies?"

"I'm just culturing the kid a little. It's an obscure interest. Let me have mine and you can have yours. I got this one on special order."

She studied the back of the cassette. "Okay... Mister know it all! Now, I'm going to let you have it! Our kid's missing this long and there you go letting a damn video game babysit him? What kind of example are you? Good grief. Did you even think to ask him about his time away? Who had him? And what happened?" She went toward Randy and wrapped her arms around him, holding him close. "I'm here. I love you, buddy."

"Mmm hmm hmm hoo," he mumbled. "Look, I learned how to whistle!"

He blew loudly, chirping like the finest calling birds in the region.

"How did you learn?" she asked.

"I don't remember."

"Why can't you tell me, Randy?" she asked, remaining tense, a side effect of her frustration with Ron's negligence. "What did they do to you?"

"I don't know." He pulled away from her.

"I couldn't get him to talk to me about one darn thing that happened," Ron said. "He just said it was dark, and a lady kept a fire lit the whole time and fed him a bunch of soup and sandwiches. That's all he remembers."

Nancy shook her head. "What about grandma's? Did she treat you well?"

"Mmm hmm."

"It never fails." She looked at Ron with narrow eyes. "I... give you the chance to bond with the kid first after being gone this long, and you treat him like dirt."

Ron interrupted. "Let's set one thing straight. You didn't give me a 'chance to bond first,' you were 'working' and couldn't swallow your pride to face your mother long enough to get him yourself."

Nancy kicked a pizza box, continuing her tear into him. "What father would be so pathetic? I don't have a clue what you do with your free time, but it sure as hell isn't keeping this place clean or taking care of anything important. I'm just thankful I can finally stop lying to people that he's living with your father in Missouri for a while. What a crock of sh..."

Ron motioned his head toward Randy. "Nancy, watch it. Young ears. I'd been meaning to tell you this," he said, his eyes growing teary, "I got the call last week. Dad died... No funeral."

"I'm sorry to hear that. No funeral? What do you mean?"

"They found his will. It explicitly requested no funeral."

"He may have been the finest of all of our parents," she said.

Ron's breath eased. "Yeah, yeah. Buttering me up at this point is useless. He's gone. Changing subjects, I'm gonna say something you want to hear."

"I'm listening."

"You've been exactly right all along," he mumbled. "I am pathetic."

She nodded her head, smiling. "Are you going to do anything to act on this conclusion that you've come to?"

"Not right now. Give me some time to sort through personal affairs."

"That figures." She kicked the side of the TV stand and it buckled. Ron ran toward it to stabilize it.

"Watch it. That's a rental!"

"Something always comes up! Wait a second. You're renting this furniture? It's particle board... that's all they're selling these days." She grabbed Ron, shaking him up in her frustration. "Randy, get your things. Ron, I want this place cleaned up, or I'll be calling child services. This is nonsense. This orangutan habitat isn't good for you or anyone else. I don't know how you can even stand it. How embarrassing!"

He backed away from Nancy, clearly offended a moment before mimicking a monkey toward Randy. "Somehow, I doubt that... Ooh... Ooh!"

"Did you even give him a shower?"

Ron made eye contact with Randy. "Yes. He's all clean"

She sniffed of Randy. "I'm not buying it."

"He did," Randy said. "I promise, mom."

"Your hair's way too greasy." She continued to inspect and smell him. "I figured grandma would have at least taken the initiative to do this while you were with her last night. With all that friggin' earth loving water conservation crap, she's probably resorting to catching it from barrels on her back porch while she smokes rolled up Bermuda. Crazy thing."

"Nancy, cool down. One day he's going to repeat some of this. I have no idea how she'll take it."

"See if I care." She moved toward the door. "When are you going to become an adult, Ron? You're too damn old to live like a preschooler."

"Come on... You know I've been playing the markets with my cashed-out retirement funds. I've got this new job. Dad's proceeds from the estate will be distributed once the attorneys get things figured out. It's gonna be okay. The dividends I've got tied up in Riverton Financial are taking care of me for now... and the house has that contract. I know, I know. I let stuff pile up a while, and, then, like a *logical* man, I clean it up in one swoop. Why take out the trash every day when they only come to pick it up once a week? It makes no difference to me."

She scoffed. "My conclusion still stands," she said, poking him in the belly. "*You* are a pig."

Ron picked up the pizza boxes from beneath the table. "While you're on your way out — since you have such an opinion, why don't you carry this to the garbage for me? Do you mind?"

Nancy lunged at Ron, cocking her head back as if she were about to headbutt him, her eyes furious. "You are a sorry person when you make excuses. You have me hating your kind right now."

Ron put his hand on her shoulder. "Nancy, pull it together. Randy's watching... I'm sorry," he sighed, looking away in self-disgust. "You're right, I am an ape... or wait... a pig."

She shoved his hand away, storming out of the room.

Randy peeked around the corner. "See you later," the boy said.

***

Nancy pulled up to the hotel — the spotlights illuminating the words OAK and HOLLOW brighter than THE or HOTEL.

The place doesn't look as good at night, she thought. *I'll have to talk to Greenwich about nighttime curb appeal.*

She unbuckled her seatbelt, sipping on a convenience store coffee she hoped would get her through the overnight shift. Putting the Caprice wagon into park, she turned around and looked at Randy.

"Why are we here?" Randy asked.

"I guess we didn't have this conversation before you disappeared on us." she said, putting her hand on Randy's knee. "I've got a job here. I've got to work tonight. I'll set you up in my basement apartment. It's even got a TV and some fancy hotel snacks in the refrigerator."

His face turned pale. "You aren't going to talk to me, anymore? Didn't you miss me? What about our house? Why was daddy in that other place? I'm scared of the basement."

"Your father and I are taking some time apart. Some other people are going to buy the house from us. Why are you scared of the basement, honey? There's nothing to be afraid of."

"Grandma's house," he said, trembling.

I swear if she... I'm going to kill her, she thought.

"What did she do to you?"

Randy looked away, pondering on the question. "Last night, she gave me a bunch of cough medicine and it made me sleepy. I woke up and she and these other old ladies carried me into her basement... They all got naked under these weird gray robes and danced around me. Chanting and laughing. One lady with a hood over her head poured blood down my throat and they covered me with dirt. When I woke up the next morning, I was back in the guest room, clean and comfortable."

"Oh, Randy... I bet you just had a bad dream."

"I thought that, too. I was perfectly clean, but grandma didn't know I still had dirt in my pockets from when they buried me. I found it when we got to the apartment that day."

You'll pay your penance alright. Snake! she thought.

"Why didn't you tell me sooner?" she asked, putting her hand on the top of his knee.

Randy covered his eyes with his hands and started to cry. "I didn't want her to die. I didn't want you to kill her."

"I would never kill her. She deserves a more painful justice. I wish you would have told me before we got over here."

"Did you guys look for me? That lady didn't want to let me out."

Nancy hesitated, a momentary guilt coming over her, "Of course, we looked for you, sweetheart. Let's go inside. We'll sit in the lobby and visit. I may have to tend to a few customers. There's a TV in there and the A/C is good and cool.

"We don't always have to watch TV. Maybe we could play a board game? You never want to do that kind of stuff with me. Grandma's right. I guess I'm too uninteresting for you."

Oh my gosh...

"Honey, you know that's not true. Sure, we can play a game. What did you have in mind?"

"Like that one grandma played with me last time?"

She squinted toward him. "Which one?"

"You know, the one where the letters float around on the board on their own when you ask it a question."

Bobbie Helbens... you are now officially dead, she thought. *Why don't I let you stamp your own damn name on a death certificate?*

CHAPTER EIGHTEEN

VIC RAMSEY walked down the street after a few hours at Bridgewater — moderately buzzed as his mind remained anxious.

I guess it's my night to check in, he thought.

Oak Hollow Lane was at the foot of Old Town Riverton, an area whose aggressive revitalization was questionable at best. Over the last few years, the area's surroundings were updated considerably, leaving many to wonder what parts of its seedy past would be recovered as old buildings came roaring back to life.

Erase what you know and start over, he thought. *We're going to start from scratch. Calhoun just slipped, that's all. Anybody who fixates too long on the same thing is bound to do the same. You have to break it up to stay healthy. Do what you can to keep your feet on the ground. It's a special assignment — an opportunity. A chance to reinvent your miserably predictable life. It might as well be 2-D and black and white, Vic. A little color never hurt anybody...*

He looked up at The Oak Hollow Hotel, a genuine beauty to its origins in its restored state – a relic to be treasured and cherished for generations. Atop the hotel, a lone American flag waved in the wind, while blocked white letters spelled out its name on the stony sides of the contrasting top level. The north and south ends were covered in double-paned windows, while the east and west remained covered in brick on the lower seven floors — a faux stucco presenting itself on the eighth. The floor was isolated — a raised enclave in the center of the building with a lone window peering to the north and another to the south. Vic jotted a few notes on his scribble pad. Each floor was lit with warm colored incandescents behind select curtains. Tall, sturdy oak trees stood in a few spots on either side of the building.

A glowing figure standing at the back of the property caught his attention as they moved behind a storage building. With curiosity piqued, he walked that way. Moving toward the back, a clanking sound rang out, but he couldn't identify where the figure went.

Not going to say anything or call out to them, he thought. *This is how the good guy usually dies.*

He walked next to the hotel, passing a parking lot of vehicles, and making a few observations on his notepad.

Too many empty spots. It speaks of arrogance. An overconfident hotelier who simply can't humble himself to drop the nightly rate, despite slow business. Maybe he wants it that way. I guess it's not my problem to figure how he affords to keep the lights on.

A silhouetted figure approached him from the opposite side of the street.

The man called over to him, "Vic, it's Livewire. We met in the bar a while back. I've got somethin' else I need to say to you."

Man, not this guy again.

"Have you just been staking the place out and waiting until I show up or what? Get to it, then. What's so important?"

"She can be bought," Livewire whispered.

"Who can be bought? With what?"

He chuckled. "That's all you need to know," he said, handing an envelope to Vic. "Give this letter to Nancy. She works in there."

"I'm not a messenger. You're a grown man. Give it to her yourself."

"I can't. I'm not goin' back in there."

"I'll read it," Vic threatened. "I hope it's nothing I shouldn't be reading."

"Suit yourself. I'm not gonna judge ya. It ain't for you, though, so it probably won't mean much." He waved at Vic and turned around, walking away and up the street. Vic's failing eyeglass prescription lost his unlikely acquaintance somewhere behind Bridgewater, about a half mile's walk from where he stood.

I have no more time for your nonsense. Just let me write my article and be on my way. I ain't no errand boy.

He walked to his Impala and sat for a few minutes. Pulling out a pint of *Old Tymer's* from the glove box, he poured it into a fuzzy canteen. He studied the cursive chicken scratch on the front of the envelope, pondering if he should read it.

MS. NANCY

I don't know her... I don't know him. Why would I care what he wrote?

He sipped on his drink, reviewing the surrounding area. Pulling out his scribble pad, he jotted the lead line to his article.

Life's too short to be meaningless. And meaningless, the Oak Hollow Hotel is not.

He could hear Dorse's hoarse voice as he studied the walls of his office in his imagination — the smell of his hot Lucky Strike and freshly printed newsprint filling his mental nasal passages.

'*What a pile of hooey, Ramsey,*' he thought. '*Is that the best you can come up with? Give me something with more substance if you want to stay on the payroll.*'

He scribbled a doodle of Dorse onto the paper, drawing him with an exaggerated plumpness and elongated chin, next to a taller, handsome version of himself. The speech balloon he drew next to his own head remained empty while he sketched his green eyed and salt and pepper mug, much more handsome than he actually was. His cartoon likeness left his hair thicker, his features more distinguished, and his waistline a sleek thirty-two.

This is stupid. New lead line...

Storied Hotel Races to Escape Troubling Past.

That'll work just fine.

He climbed out of the car, stumbling toward the hotel's entrance — his blurred vision growing worse with his increased inebriation.

THE OAK HOLLOW HOTEL — ERECTED 1926 BY DON WASSERMAN... MAY OUR FOLLY NEVER LEAD US ASTRAY.

FOR W.W.

1926-1958, Restored: DEC. 1985-DEC. 1990, by the RIVERTON PRECINCT THREE COUNCIL AND THE GREENWICH FAMILY ESTATE.

PROPRIETOR - J. GREENWICH

You've seen the outside. Now it's time to see the inside.

CHAPTER NINETEEN

NANCY HELBENS stood still, studying the cherry wood atop the lobby desk.

The day Greenwich sees the ashy underside of this will be the day I'm packing my bags.

She peeled off the date from the Motor Trend desk calendar, Monday, July 28th, 1991.

The wood paneled television across from the lobby played a repeat of *The Tonight Show*. Johnny Carson was on a rant, but she missed the lead up to the punchline.

A man loitered out front of the hotel several minutes, studying the signage. She assumed him to be a drunk or a criminal. After some time, he stumbled in through the revolving door. His gait was distinct, almost distracting.

I've seen you at the deli before, haven't I? she thought.

Taking a deep breath, she greeted him. "Good evening. Welcome to The Oak Hollow Hotel. How can I assist you? Do you have a reservation?"

He slapped his credit card on the counter, reeking of strong booze. His greasy hair made him appear older than he was. The aged pattern in his tie, a nod to a man whose working-class days began in the early sixties and were likely to fade into the sunset with the impending new millennium. He didn't acknowledge Nancy in any proper way, he merely made his demand.

"I want a room. Some place I can hear myself think. The hotel doesn't have issues with paperthin walls, right?"

She glanced at him a moment, pondering upon the question before replying, "It depends. The sixth floor is quiet. Way quieter than it should be. I'll get you set up right away if that suits you? How about a nice city-view room?"

He nodded his head. "Six is good... perfect in fact."

"The rate's $179 a night. Does that suit you okay?"

"Be my guest," he muttered, reaching in his back pocket for his billfold. "Book me for four nights and give me some space."

This is a real rip-off, guy. Whatever...

"What?"

"Sure. That's fine. Book me. I don't care. I'm good for it."

"Fair enough. I'll just need you to fill out this form and sign off on the liability and damage waivers, and I'll make a copy of your driver's license."

She handed a pen to the man, pushing the form toward him. He shoved it away.

"No IDs. The Visa will have to do. You have a Bic? I like the black-inked ones."

She looked at the cup of pens on the corner of the lobby counter.

Never paid attention to the brands. There was a Paper Mate, a Uniball, and a red, chewed on Ticonderoga in the cup but that was it.

The tone in the man's voice grew sarcastic, "It's a simple 'yes' or 'no' question. Do you or don't you have one?"

"I'll have to check in the back."

She turned around to approach the office just behind the lobby, before he interrupted. "Forget it. I have one. I just try to use it sparingly. It's my ticket to livelihood." He reached into his pocket, holding it in his left hand and running it across the paperwork as he glossed over the disclaimers and agreements, mumbling to himself.

What are you rambling about? she thought.

Nancy referenced the hotel policy manual for situations such as this. The former proprietor, Don Wasserman, had been thorough in his forethought many years earlier.

"Okay," she said. "Well, I'll just need you to write your social security number on the form since you don't have a license, black ink please."

The man scoffed. "You guys sure do a lot of C-Y-A. Don't you?"

She smiled. "Screening our guests is critical to keeping trouble out of here."

He waved her off, walking over to the coffee pot, and pouring the caffeinated beverage into a paper cup stamped with a gold embossed hotel logo.

"How fresh is this?" he called from across the room.

She looked up from the manual. "It's still percolating. Isn't it?"

Gawking at the reply, he said, "That's vague. Coffee can do that for hours. What gives?" He swigged the drink quickly before becoming choked up.

She called across the lobby, "Are you okay, sir?"

"What is this? A strong Central American brew?"

"Actually, it's native to the region. Our own house blend."

He talked to himself a moment, something unintelligible before replying. "Oh really? It's got a hint of sweetness to it. I think that's the water more than the coffee grounds."

He approached the counter, sniffing toward the cup and the lingering scent of the potent drink.

"Alright, sir. The elevator is just down that hall. I've got you in six-o-five. Here's the key. Make yourself at home. I've just run your card for half the length of your stay. We'll do the second round if you check out."

The man returned an empty stare. "You mean, when...?"

Well said, Nancy, she thought. *Well said. Your customer facing skills are unmatchable.*

She blushed. "Yes. I'm sorry... *when* you check out. Can I help you with your bag?"

He pursed his lips, taking the key from her. "I prefer my privacy. Thank you."

He pulled out a letter from his bag, hoisting it toward her. "I have a delivery for you."

She shook her head.

"Just take it and let me get on the elevator."

"Okay?" she said, reaching for it. "It was just repaired. The ride might be bumpy."

As he climbed on, she studied his dark eyes as the door closed. He wedged his hand in to stop it.

"Six-o-five is down the hall and to the right once you get up there."

"Okay, thank you."

CHAPTER TWENTY

Dropping his small travel bag on the corner table, VIC RAMSEY picked up a piece of the hotel stationary, studying it with care before looking at the room that surrounded. He twisted the ceramic blue lamp on, yanking the Bic from his pocket, and jotting his first impression.

THE OAK HOLLOW HOTEL — RIVERTON, TEXAS

Am I resorting to grading a hotel by the stationery it supplies its guests? Yes, I am. Its pallet speaks of an institution trying hard to find its identity... washed out in a shade of gray, an appetite for yellow, but too murky to identify as ivory. What's that color? Ecru. The stationery is a mild and warm ecru. As for its textural consistency, it's a cheap, cross threaded cardstock from an office supply store, nothing special. The hotel's messy O.H. crest is stamped slightly off center, as if it's too much to outsource to a professional. I kind of like it, despite its leaning toward human error. Maybe the hourly worker in the lobby was buzzed when they stamped this one. The wood-paneled Zenith is a perfect match to the one in the common area with a few less dust bunnies. The remote is bolted to a cheap end table on the right side of the bed. This leads me to my first question.

Is the Oak Hollow Hotel just another poser four star doing the typical smoke and mirrors routine?

It makes me think of several other peculiar hotel restorations I've read about across the Lone Star State. I can only assume they're financed by half-hearted government grants, paying it backward to native tribes robbed years earlier.

I guess it helps the politicians sleep better at night. I'm thinking they're more concerned about a ride in a posh Mercedes and a J-Crew getup to show off downtown than righting the wrongs of the past, though. At first glance, Oak

Hollow well may be predestined to join the ranks of common two-star motor-lodge commodities housed in the façade of a hotel building... Not to worry, ladies and germs, the stale donuts and coffee before nine, and the drive-up bulletproof partition are waiting with a chain-smoking hospitalitarian sitting just inside, and offering you a false sense of security to repel his invisible 'sleaze' factor. I've got nothing against Days Inn or La Quinta, but I hate hotels that try to fake it. Just do us all a favor, and be yourself, please. Once upon a time, these places carried a unique identity pointing to their past. That is quickly becoming an out-of-focus memory in the rearview, folks. If you're looking for original, a quick perusal of the area's hotels will all point you back to The Oak Hollow Hotel, the lone institution yet to sell itself to a multinational corporation that franchises its rooms more predictable than a soggy Happy Meal. I like the boutique... the novelty of mom-and-pop run franchises. I'm hoping Oak Hollow leaves me pleasantly surprised prior to checkout.

Standing up, Vic looked around the room. Moving toward the outer edge, he ran his fingernails across the walls of six-o-five with care before swiftly walking back to the table and continuing to write.

The walls are textured with sheetrock beneath and what I'm assuming to be two layers of forgettable wallpaper print. I'm unclear why anyone in the industry finds veneer an appealing or marketable quality. You don't have to look very far to see it's a farce. The northwest corner of the room already looks to be peeling where the walls come together. The side effect, a glimpse at the ugly forest green the restoration crew failed to remove to install a marginally better paisley printed tortilla tone. Yikes!

The king-sized bed is a pillowtop with an extra eggcrate, draped in a bedspread with O.H. embroidered across the outer layer of the gold toned comforter and lined with two sets of sheets. It very well may be the highlight of the room and its elusive owner's largest investment. Each bedpost stretches to the ceiling like a desperate hand reaching from an unseen abyss. The brochure in the lobby promises antique wood salvaged from a fire that nearly robbed the hotel of its connection with the distant past. The room's distinguished drapery is the perfect blend of Texas vintage and contemporary.

The refrigerator is stocked with three bottles of pulpy orange juice, a can of the less than palatable Flitz, sample bottles of Old Tymer's, and an assortment of fruits in a plastic container. Whether they need refrigerated, I'm unclear. I think I'll work my way through all of it before the night's over. My dull review of the hotel should be through within the hour. That's all for now.

-VR

***

Vic popped open the *Old Tymer's* — his lips twinging as the alcohol burned the outside.

Let's have a look at the city-view the clerk seemed so enthused to offer.

Moving toward the window to peek behind it at the less than symmetrical Riverton skyline, the window revealed an enclosed outer area on the floor.

Hmm...

Efforts to open the window proved useless. It was bolted shut. Pressing his face nearer to the glass to study it, a rush of cool air hit the back of his neck.

I'm not alone, am I?

The patterns on the carpet on the other side of the glass were primitive — the outer walls, stacked gray cinder blocks lined with a thick mortar. The lights on the ceiling in the hall reflected a reddish hue. As he threw the curtains closed, there was a tap on the glass. He clicked off the lamp and collapsed on the bed, opting to ignore it.

Closing his eyes, his final thoughts wandered.

It's just been a long day. You need to slow down for a bit. The dark room will help. I bet it's just an unconventional fire-escape route. The Deus ex machina... Cheap, manufactured thrills will not define my success anymore. I'm a new kind of professional. Journalists should never be pigeonholed. We change like the seasons — our inspiration arriving in varying forms and fashions.

He nodded away to sleep, struggling to identify if inebriation was the culprit bogging him down.

***

A commotion came from the glass, as if it were being slid open from the outside. Vic leaned over and flicked the Zenith on as its glow illuminated the room. Johnny Carson played on repeat.

The joke didn't get any funnier the second time, or the third. I never connect with that self-assured humor.

He changed the channel as an old man walked dirt roads with malnourished children in a third-world country as their mother poured murky water into cups.

Looks more like water from a marshy bog in the bayou than anything worth swallowing. God help 'em.

The voice on the television was washed out with some sappy synthesizer work as the old man's voice grew emotional and the camera zoomed in on the poor children's deprivation of fair sustenance.

"For just $19.99 a month, you can buy yourself peace of mind, knowing that you paid to purify the water for four families."

Lies. Lies. Lies. If peace of mind were that cheap, the entire world would have clean water. What's your CEO's annual salary?

For the moment, whatever was happening on the other side of the glass remained postponed. He was too tired to pay it anymore attention. He drifted to sleep.

CHAPTER TWENTY-ONE

After sleeping off the long night shift, NANCY HELBENS called her mother, Bobbie. She looked around the room, hoping for something to distract her and calm her as her heart beat faster and faster. The only thing her eyes could gravitate to was the empty bar, which did nothing for her while unstocked.

I'm not ready to talk to you... I'm too angry.

There were a few extended trills before she answered.

"Hello?"

"Mom, it's Nancy. I know we haven't talked in a while, but I have something I need to get off my chest. Are you available?"

"Nancy, I wasn't expecting your call. I was wondering why you sent the deadbeat to pick up Randy. The babysitter that dropped him off was gone before I could see them. There was just a tap on the door and he was out there standing in the rain, his red hair wet, and his clothes drenched. I was glad to see our sweet boy, though. We..."

Nancy interrupted. "I wasn't expecting to make this call. I don't want to cover anything else over the telephone. Meet me at Corner Brothers Deli."

"In Old Town Riverton?"

Nancy sighed loudly. "You know good and well where it is."

"What's this about?"

"Mom, I'm sorry, not going to talk about this any further over the telephone. Meet me at 2 p.m. Deal?"

"I'll check my schedule."

Nancy scoffed. "I know you've got nothing better to do than crochet or watch the daytime soaps. Get your miserable butt over and spend a few minutes with me. Don't worry, it won't be long."

The line disconnected.

***

Nancy camped out in her favorite booth. Getting comfortable while her new book remained out of reach. The longer it marinated, the more her fury with Bobbie intensified. She sipped her coffee with a fist clenched as her mother came in the door, never bothering to wave or get her attention. Instead, she stared at the back of the booth just across until Bobbie waddled over and sat down.

Nancy crossed her arms. "Aren't you going to order something?"

"I've got no appetite... I see you've still got yours."

"I don't even have a plate, mom," Nancy said, gritting her teeth a moment. "Give me one good reason I shouldn't splash this coffee in your bulimic face?"

Bobbie shook her head. "Nancy, don't!"

"That's not what we're here to talk about. Is it, mom?"

Bobbie shifted her weight across the booth as it squeaked. "So, what are we here to talk about?"

"You know... Randy."

Bobbie's face grew pale. "Dear gracious... did something happen?"

"You tell me... What did you do to him the other night?"

She sighed as her body trembled. "It's just my tremor, Nancy. Don't mind me. It was a simple night. We turned on a children's program — I think it was a Donald Duck rerun. I fed him a TV dinner, and then I put him to bed. That's it. Ron was already there the next morning before I had any time to do anything else."

"Are you sure that's all?" Nancy asked, glaring at her mother.

"Why wouldn't it be? I've got nothing against Randy."

She dropped her fist to the table. "Against Randy? But you do against me... If you even had half a cent of credibility, I might take the bullshit answer. Not this time, Bobbie."

Bobbie's eyes widened. "Watch it. Don't you dare call me by my first name again! You townwhore eyesore..."

Oh, I could just kill you, Nancy thought.

"What did you ever have against me?" Nancy asked. "All I ever tried to be for you and for dad was perfect and agreeable. I could never meet your expectations. Could I?"

"For one, you were supposed to be a boy, Nancy. I always wanted a boy. We prayed that way for weeks, but that couldn't change fate. I lost hope in believing in anything more meaningful after that."

"I'm sorry to disappoint you with my... *existence*. I didn't mean to put you out."

"You don't understand and you never will. Your father just lied and manipulated you day in and day out to make himself look better than me. A textbook narcissist."

"Sure he did... What were you, mom?" Nancy said, splashing her mother in the face with her lukewarm coffee.

"Ah!" Bobbie's face soured, as she grabbed some napkins from the table to wipe it off.

"Is your memory getting temperamental or what?" Nancy asked. "How many damn times did you shove sand down my throat and cinch me up in the tightest corset you could find to squeeze my rolls in? Were you too proud a witch to have a fat kid? I never overindulged as a child. You wouldn't let me. You sat there on your lazy delusional ass, warping my head with your otherworldly mantras. Guess what, mom? I'm still screwed up."

The manager of the restaurant approached the table, nodding toward Nancy and then speaking to Bobbie. "Excuse me, ma'am. I didn't see you order anything. I don't welcome people to loiter around if they're not going to order."

"Did you pay him off to say this?" Bobbie asked, wiping more coffee from her face and hair as she glared at Nancy.

"Of course not, mom. You've got such a paranoid mind."

"Ma'am, what will it be? What can we get you?" the manager asked.

"A cup of coffee," Bobbie said, "Black as night. You know what I mean. Don't you?"

"Fine," he said, walking away from the table.

Bobbie shook her head at Nancy. "I don't know what you're getting at. This is all a shock to me. I want you to be able to trust me, honey."

"Don't you dare call me, honey," Nancy said, clamping her lips together tighter.

"People are staring," Bobbie muttered. "This is getting embarrassing."

"Great... Here I go again, humiliating and embarrassing you. Do you have a particular time in mind that you just can't let go?"

Bobbie never hesitated. "You bled all over my mother's knitted blanket. I had to teach you a lesson."

"What you did to me was abuse me. You were too damn busy drinking the days away with your space-cadet friends, 'keeping in touch with the earth.' I never had a normal day, mom — ever."

"Oh, Nancy..."

"Finally struck a plastic feeling in you? Your crocodile tears are *so* pretty, mom. Good... Guess what? It's time to face the wrath and see what a failure you were to yourself... to dad... and to me."

"This is too much. I knew it was a mistake coming over here," Bobbie said, moving toward the outside of the booth. "I've got to go to the bathroom."

"Don't bother. I'm leaving. I hope you sleep better tonight. Make sure not to choke yourself shoving too many friggin' Prozac's down your throat. Someone might miss you."

Bobbie started slamming her head on the table. Nancy stormed out of the restaurant, opting to sit on the bench outside to wait for her.

The restaurant manager walked Bobbie out, her eyes still livid, and her forehead bruising. "Listen here," he said. "I don't want to see any more of this post-menopausal nonsense in my restaurant anymore. Either you pull yourself together, or I'll ban you from eating in here. You understand me?"

Nancy looked at him. "I'm sorry. It won't happen again. Will it, mother?"

"I suppose not," she remarked, staring at Nancy with evil eyes.

"You best get on your way, ladies. Go find you one of those peace and love gardens and hug it out." He walked back into the restaurant, shaking his head as the two women sat by one another in stone silence.

Nancy lit a cigarette.

Bobbie scoffed. "Look at you shoving the cancer sticks in your mouth like they're candy. No wonder..."

"No wonder, what?" Nancy asked.

"Nothing..."

"Mom, I think its best that we cut our ties."

"It's no skin off my back. My life is better with you out of my hair."

Nancy puffed on her cigarette. "Randy won't be seeing you again, either. You want to know why I called you down here?"

"To chew me out for all my missteps and tell me what a perfect mother that *you've* become?"

Nancy scoffed. "Is that what you think of me, mom? I'm disappointed you see me that shallow and hollow. You never cared, did you? You never had your boy and all I am is a reminder of a past regret."

Bobbie's voice was shaky. "Nancy, I tried, honey. You were never an easy child."

"The only thing easy about either of us was you, and the way you were with dad before you were smart enough to count the cost of screwing around."

Bobbie continued to cry.

Nancy motioned toward herself. "You got what you paid for. The reason I called you was to chew you out for messing with Randy. Did you practice on him?"

"Practice?" Bobbie looked away for a second. "What are you talking about, Nancy?"

"You know what I'm talking about. Don't think I forgot about your casual ladies club. The poor kid told me he's got memories tattooed in his little mind, seeing a bunch of old hags dance around him in gray smocks and chant at him. I bet you candled him, too. Was he impure like I was? He just turned seven years old. You think, because I came from the scourge of your loins, that he did, too? By proxy?" Nancy said, jabbing the burning tip of her cigarette on her mother's hand.

"Ah! Don't do that!" Bobbie shrieked. "You're crazy! I can't talk anymore. You're delusional and you always were. I never laid a hand on him. I stopped poking around with all that stuff after... after your father died." She stood up and walked toward her Taurus.

"I bet you did. You killed him. I don't know what cop you bought off..."

"Mitch was on a path to self-destruction," she said, starting the vehicle. "I liberated him." Bobbie closed her car door and drove away.

Whatever, mom.

CHAPTER TWENTY-TWO

After sobering up, the next morning, a silhouetted shadow went across VIC RAMSEY's room. The clock radio came on, waking him with a worldbeat, new age number from *Enigma*.

"Who's in here?" he whispered. "This is a private room."

The character lingered, standing in the area nearest the lavatory as Vic's breathing elevated.

"I asked you a question. Are you going to say anything? I'm just here to do a hotel review. I don't want any trouble."

The character's silence chilled him.

"Enough of this."

Vic moved across the corner room, pulling the curtains open on the opposite window. His jacket hung on a coat rack near the lavatory, assuming this to be the mistaken figure.

This was it?

Moonlight shined through the room's south window. He tucked the curtains open and studied the street. Looking below, an older woman moved her house on wheels, a glorified grocery basket with a laundry rack mounted atop. A short man took a smoke break outside the Bridgewater Restaurant. Another pulled up to the front of the hotel in a limousine. Vic sat at the desk, jotting a few more notes on the previous night's discoveries.

Well, I'd be telling a fib if I didn't notate six-o-five's bizarre overnight qualities. It's not the darkness in the room I'm referring to, but rather, the unwelcome feeling in the back of my throat that makes me feel like I'm not alone. I can't run from it. Not with alcohol, smokes, or the fine tipped quill of my Bic with exaggerated wordplay. The cinder blocked walls outside the east side of my room last night, hinted at another world I could see but could never reach. Is that what hell feels like? One step outside of something greater, a glaring reminder of the folly we can never escape? Which side of the glass am I on now and which side do I want to be on later?

–VR

Falling to the floor in a fit of unexpected convulsions, Vic grabbed at his chest as if a piece of his heart was stripped away. A voice in his head talked loudly as distant memories threw him into an unfamiliar past.

I'm lying in a hospital bed. Mom and dad are there. My sister's there. My younger brother's there. I hear the beeps of the heart monitor, but I'm unable to recall what happened or why. I sense a frustration in my parents, like whatever I've done has violated their trust. I pass out. They're mumbling to one another and my father says, "He's a screw up, Willow. Just like I was."

My mother doesn't argue, instead she turns away from me and my father and starts speaking to the air in an unknown Pentecostal tongue I can't understand. My father ignores her. Something's clearly been wrong with her for years, but he doesn't know how to help. My brother and sister are more infatuated with the honey roasted peanuts from the vending machine than anything else, and sadly they're all oblivious to mom's growing decline.

I try to sit up. A doctor comes in, sedating me again as I work to speak.

"He's never going to be the same, folks," the doctor declares. "How high was that tree again?"

"About twenty feet," my mother responds, biting at the nail on her index finger compulsively.

"Trauma to the head is a tricky thing," the doctor says. "We stopped the bleeding quickly. But his brain may never quite be the same. Don't be discouraged. We're resilient beings, and the brain rewires itself in its own special ways in a lot of these incidents. The rebuilding process is variable, though. It's hard for me to speculate. Your son is just going to be different than you remember. He's blessed with a second chance. I wish his friend would have been so lucky. What was her name again?"

I can't hear my mother's response to the doctor. It fades away. The doctor's lab coat looks like it's getting longer and longer, and the floor beneath him disappears. He's floating there while the rest stand around him. Mom's mouth moves, but I'm drifting away. My mind wanders as the sedative takes hold and I see myself falling from the oak tree in slow motion. A dark cloaked figure lunges toward me as I near the ground, and then I see a bright glowing figure sitting below to pad the fall for me. The dark cloaked one slams my little friend's head to the ground twice as hard, and her spirit floats away. There's no scream, just a life separated from this world far too soon and well before any of us would have hoped.

I recall the moment. We climbed up the tall ladder dad had forgotten to lock away in the garage. She stood on my shoulders to reach the top.

"Come on up," she said. "You can see everything from up here!"

I leap toward the sky, grabbing the branch to hoist myself up. It snaps.

The convulsion stopped and Vic Ramsey regained consciousness, a bottle of *Old Tymer's* having spilled all over his shirt.

You're becoming a drunk, hung over loser, again. Aren't you? Get in the shower, and sort yourself out. Look at you, reeking of booze and failure.

Moving toward the lavatory, he twisted the hot water knob about seventy-five percent of the way and the cold water to ten percent. Thirty seconds passed and the water temperature was comfortable to the touch.

Ah, the comforts of western civilization.

He moved the clock radio to the lavatory as *Peter Gabriel* chirped through the speaker.

The steam in the room filled the air, fogging the mirror quickly after the fact, a 3, 6, and 9, showing beneath. The rush of water ran down Vic's back as he searched his mind for the roots of his memory. The shower water turned black, spewing all over his skin, before it cleared after a few seconds.

I guess it's been a while since anyone's used the shower. The plumbing needs a good tune up.

He turned the water off, grabbing a towel from the rack. Dabbing the skin on his arm where the black oil remained, the color in his skin rubbed onto it.

What the heck is going on?

He continued drying his body with the towel, noting the select areas where the black water had touched his skin, and an unknown vulnerability to pigment discoloration. Exiting the lavatory, he dressed into his charcoal suit and psyched himself up.

It's just my imagination, he thought. *That's all. Pull yourself together. Time to check out while you're still ahead. You don't need four days to do a thorough review. One night was plenty.*

Chest pain overwhelmed him as his heart raced and he grabbed at his numbing left arm.

Pop a nitro pill, Vic. It's not the end yet. Fifty-three isn't the year for you to go.

He mellowed upon taking the medication, sitting at the foot of the bed.

That's better.

Grabbing his bag a moment, he dropped it back on the bed as he walked toward the hand scribbled review on the corner desk.

Don't want to forget this...

Walking out the door and into the corridor to the elongated sixth floor hallway, disorientation overwhelmed. Looking toward the carpet, sun and moon patterns shifted into varying shapes of bones. The shapes looked to jump through the carpet seams toward him, knocking him backwards.

CHAPTER TWENTY-THREE

VIC RAMSEY awoke in a darkened hallway, its distinct red glow reflecting upon his face. Moving toward a window on the inner wall, his efforts to open it proved futile.

What's going on here?

The space's cinder blocked outer walls made the area claustrophobic and sterile. Approaching the southeastern corner of the floor, he walked down the hallway toward its end. An old shower curtain covered an area just behind it. Looking around for a moment, he yanked the curtain abruptly. Five skeletons sat in lawn chairs spaced apart at equal distances on the outer wall. The sixth chair was empty. They sat stiff, appearing reinforced. A jar of bone paste rested atop a neighboring barrel.

Don't suppose that's medical grade. These skeletons are remarkably intact, though... hmm.

Unconventional to his typical self, he called out, "I guess this is the part where I'm supposed to sit and let you decimate the skin off my body to match with the others?"

A shushing sound came down the hall as another figure came toward him.

"Is there someone there?" he asked.

A large man with thinning red hair approached. While Vic expected his heart to pound through his throat, adrenaline failed to engage.

The man's voice was creaky and unused in recent times, "We're just around for a short period each night. Don't ruin it for the rest."

Vic moved toward him. "What do you mean?"

The large fellow stepped back into the shadows. "I mean that this... conjured existence is hexed by time."

Vic squinted, struggling to focus. "Hexed by time?"

The man's voice became a graveled whisper, "Three hours a night — from 2-5 a.m."

Vic rocked his heels, placing his hand against the outer cinder block wall. "What about the rest?"

The wall scalded him — his hand sizzling, but the pain never lingering. He pulled away from it, looking to the one he spoke to for validation. The smell of the burned flesh made him gag.

"You didn't feel it anymore, did you? You're as good as dead. Don't expect a way out..."

He motioned toward Vic to move further through the hallway. The red glow surrounding them brightened as they moved further through the darkened corridor.

"How are you talking to me, then?" Vic asked.

"I'm no better off. Simply experienced. This place has my number, too."

"Your number? What are you saying?"

"It's hungry for wayward souls," the man said, his voice dropping to a whisper.

"What? The hotel? That just seems like a pretentious bunch of poppycock."

The man shook his head. "Think that way if you want. Hell burns hot, and the cold, dark world gets colder. Trust me. Pick your poison."

Vic studied the man's glowing eyes. "So, why bother with me? I'm not that interesting."

"It's time I admit to you I hopped. I stayed too long."

"Hopped? What does that mean?" Vic asked, moving toward the hotel room window nearest him. He leaned toward it, trying to pull it open.

"Don't do that," he said. "Hopping... it's a bit esoteric — a form of astral-projection. We take on the form of those that we want for the interval. They're usually none the wiser. You were different. I saw your defining moments and was intrigued, but I messed up... and then, you saw a piece of my past. It's not supposed to go that way."

"What are you saying? The interval? You make it sound so technical."

"It is technical," the red-headed man answered. "That's all that's bargained for, and if we overstay our welcome, we're forced to move beyond."

"Move beyond what? A meaningless, finite existence after death?"

"With an outlook like that, your stone will roll away quickly." He pulled up a lawn chair, motioning to Vic to sit down.

"I don't follow."

"It's an ancient concept," the man continued, "From the inherited wisdom of Solomon... 'before the silver cord can be broken or the golden bowl is crushed... the dust will return to the earth as it was and the spirit returns to the God who gave life.'"

"What does that even mean?"

The man motioned toward the spine of the skeleton. "Our silver cord isn't broken." He pointed to the skull. "Our golden bowl houses matter elsewhere after the soul has moved on."

Vic made a whistling sound, pointing to his head and rolling his eyes. "Whatever you say... What are these skeletons doing here? Who were they? Why are they?"

The man spoke softly, "I thought *you* would have known more...."

"You did? I'm Vic Ramsey." He extended his hand to shake the man's. Its texture seemed inhuman, but there was no proper comparison.

"I know. Chris Wilkerson. Nice to meet you."

"What happened to you? Wilkerson, you say?"

"Yeah," he said, slicking his hair back. "I used to own this building, 'til it took everything I knew as normal and made it abnormal."

"That sounds like the making of a great autobiography."

"Maybe so. Things have gotten... complicated," Wilkerson said, motioning toward Vic to follow him through the hallway. They walked past the outer windows of several rooms as the glow of lights and televisions shined through the curtains in the wee hours of the night. "What drew you here? This old hotel has its share of skeletons in the closet. No pun intended. I'm not sure why they resurrected it. Every iteration I've ever seen seems cursed."

"Cursed? Isn't this 'afterlife' you're talking about some kind of blessing for the worthy?"

"We're each entitled to our opinion, but I think it's too early for someone like *you* to make such an assumption. I wasn't expecting the sixth seat to be filled again this week."

"Sixth seat?" Vic asked. "That empty chair over there?"

Chris stroked his cheeks, stepping back from Vic. "It's empty because you refuse to acknowledge what is there. You're no more flesh and blood than any of the rest of us. How about a change of scenery? We have thirty minutes 'til time's up..."

"What are you proposing?"

Chris smiled. "Don't really have much need to eat anymore, but we still can. How about a sandwich?"

"What's the point?" Vic asked.

"You'll see in due time. Six-o-nine has a hot plate and a lunchmeat and cheese rack in there. These people are a drag to watch, though. You only thought your life was uninteresting."

"Uninteresting?" Vic asked. "You told me you hopped into my head, didn't you?"

"I just jogged a memory from your past to see what defined you. No big deal."

Vic crossed his arms. "No, actually I feel violated. It's a huge deal. I think it's about time I grow out of thinking that way. It's more harmful than helpful."

"Don't worry," Chris said, piping something into the room from a neighboring tank. It spewed a whooshing sound as a chemical entered the air.

"What is that?"

"Wait here a minute... It's just something to knock them out flatter while we're in there. They won't remember." Chris moved toward the hot plate and cheese board and prepped the sandwiches.

Vic climbed in through the window of six-o-nine. Two guests were asleep side by side as a television repeated the infomercial for clean water at a high volume.

The man mumbled something, startling Vic.

His wife rolled over and said, "You're sleep talking again, aren't you? Why aren't you taking your sleeping pills?"

Chris kept quiet, lobbing the sandwich into his mouth and munching.

"Mmm... there you go. Here's your half, Vic. It's good."

The older woman spoke, "Ugh... your breath? Did you eat more of that lunchmeat and cheese?"

The man didn't respond.

Chris and Vic walked back across the room toward the window and climbed out.

They moved toward the outer halls on the east side of the sixth floor, sitting down at a card table.

Vic studied the skeletons just across. "Some of this is just too intriguing. Help me understand..."

"There are consequences for hopping... side-effects. Their most vivid memories... you see them and they burn themselves into your mind's eye like they're your own, disorienting your reality. Usually it's innocent things, a cotton candy at the carnival, a first kiss, when daddy taught you to ride your bike, a cherished vacation..."

"That doesn't sound so bad."

"It's not... until you find one that celebrates their worst memories as if they were their best. Judge carefully so you don't hop into the essence of pure evil. There are people... guests of this hotel, which fit that category."

"How do you know the difference?" Vic asked.

Chris adjusted one of the skeletons straighter. "People are mostly good, most of the time. It's the ones that seem good all the time that you have to watch out for. They're always hiding something. You know, something close to the vest... and quite often, they're quickest to highlight that. It's a character flaw. You'll learn to watch for it in due time. This property is disrupted in troubling ways... and you haven't even been to the tunnel yet, have you?"

"The tunnel?" Vic asked, hesitating a moment as he thought back to his bizarre night earlier in the year. "No. I guess not."

"Alright, then. Think of this place as Eden... if you ever went to Sunday school, even once, you'll recall the Tree of Knowledge... and the simple warning... Don't go."

"You're not doing a very good job at repelling me with cryptic commentary," Vic said. "It just makes me want to go in there more."

"That's because she's trying to beckon you there. You could be the swing vote."

"She? What do you mean, swing vote?"

"The old witch in the tunnel is stronger than the rest. There are two of us and three of them. It's the balance of power," Chris said.

"Witch? Okay?" Vic said, his eyes narrowing.

"Have you ever heard the myth of the Creeper... the lore of the Curioso? Oak Hollow is only one iteration... the aftermath of a devastating past. We'll do some practice 'hopping' in these skeletons. She's an odd one. I've never gotten a good read on her, but she's amassed incredible power."

"I'm still intrigued... If I do go into the tunnel, who do we answer to? What gives? From what you're explaining to me, I'm as good as dead. I might as well live a little while I can."

"Live a little? You can't think that way anymore," Chris said. "Manmade limits are a thing of the past."

"So, what's my 'present'? What do I have to keep me going?"

"The best I've gathered... The native properties are now cursed. Too much unjust blood spilled. We're stuck in a dimension between the mystical and the conscious. Come here and I'll teach you to hop. Lunge toward that third skeleton and we'll travel together. Grab the shoulder. I'll admit, this is personal, and I've never done this with anyone else before, but you've already done it once. That's me... or what's left of me. You'll hear my thoughts, feel my emotions. It's a transformative experience... it's even weirder when you're reliving your own. You can't change anything. You just watch it play out over again like a movie. Grab hold of the third skeleton, the right shoulder. You can visit the tunnel through the hop with minimal consequence."

"Okay?" Vic said, scrunching his nose. "This is a little weird... How am I talking to you if this is your skeleton?"

"Don't ask me anything else. Just experience it for yourself."

***

I'm being carried down a dark corridor. It feels so familiar, and yet I have no recollection why I feel this way. The figure carries me with care and concern. I'm just trying to decide if this is an Abraham and Isaac situation where I'm about to be tossed onto a flaming altar, hoping and praying for unspeakable mercy, or if there are greener, brighter pastures ahead. If I'm going by the tempo and the demeanor of the one doing the carrying, it feels peppy and less stiff, which I'd like to think is a good sign. What do I know? What am I, really? Who is he?

There's a well ahead. An underground well? What's going on now? My memory's amuck since... I've got nothing. What happened? The figure's voiceless, but my subconscious tells me we're connected. He pitches me in like a lucky penny and the water envelops me. I'm conscious, but I can't move. I hope he knows something I don't because the whole fight-or-flight thing isn't kicking in yet. My breath never elevates. The strange part is, I feel numb. There's no fight pushing me to free myself. Everything flashes in front of me at a rapid pace as the water forms around me and I hit the bottom of the well. I look up and see cloudy water and four other figures dancing around on either side of it. Another disproportionate hand reaches in to pull me out. I search for the willpower to move, but I still don't seem to have it. I'm lost in a sea of racing thoughts as memories flood my mind — déjà vu surrounding me while I remain submerged. The well brightens unexpectedly and I'm caught reflecting on a fractured piece of my childhood. My first lucid thought since my... awakening. I guess that's what we'll call it.

I'm finally waking, my anxiety triggers in motion. As if time stands still, I reach up to take the hand, and I'm yanked up out of the well... the spring, as a rib is jammed into my body. The abruptness to the ascent startles me as I gulp a huge amount of the liquid.

The Spring of Life. That's what this place is. It was bone dry, the last I saw it.

I can't reach the surface soon enough.

I arrive to the area and see the four other figures continuing a ritual. The sweet taste of the spring's water runs down my throat, and I'm thrown against the wall. Before I can make out the faces of the others, the walls bend toward me, and my ugly mug is pressed further and further into the ground until I can no longer breathe. He hoists me into a furnace. The scratchy and whiny voice is back again, and there's nowhere for me to run or hide as the flames engulf what's left of my body. It's Creeper Joe. His skin ever so pale. I know he can't be there. It's a test. It has to be a memory. Here I am desperate to run away from my past and to start anew, and this is what's coming back to me?

I see my past... as a mortal. His voice terrifies me to my core, "Yeah. So that's when I put them in the furnace and admired their shrieks of terror. It was quite satisfying. The smell of searing flesh... the sounds of shrieking sinners... and the retribution for the worst kinds of people to walk this beautiful earth."

There I am with him, sitting like a fool, and nodding my head at him like I grasp what he's saying. Something's not right about the memory, it's modified. Certainly not the way it actually happened. I smell myself — burning, burning, burning. This is pure misery. I can't feel the pain. I just see it as it chars away at my body. I'm pulled out of the furnace as Creeper Joe's laugh reverberates through the tunnel.

Heh-heh!

He cuts into my arm, but no blood spills. My body's now a lifeless shell.

He smiles and says, "the tables have turned, Chris. It's time to take you to school."

Before I can respond, he becomes distracted, running down the tunnel before he crumbles away. Is this how it happened? I don't know. The four other figures near the spring wave me onward. Each of them are seated on large stones that surround the spring. They point to an empty one as if expecting me to sit down. I'm in no pain from the furnace. As I study my flesh, I see it's no longer charred, instead it's restored. I take a seat and study the spring's waterfall as it cascades to the water below. Before I can speak, I see the Shadow standing there. He's the link between each of us and this place — whether forsaken or blessed, it's unclear.

Studying the motion of the waterfall, I drift away, further from myself than I've ever been.

***

Vic stared toward Chris pulling away from the third skeleton, three shades lighter than before the hop.

"That's about all of that I can take," he said. "How about a change of scenery?"

"Try reliving it over and over. It's a real trip! Let me take you down the hall. I've still got some educational materials compiled from my days doing downtown ghost tours after dark if you want an attention diversion."

A flashing sign with purple neon cursive lined the wall, INFORMATION CENTER.

"This looks awfully official to be stored away in a forgotten storage wing."

"I just ripped this off of Greenwich. He didn't need it," Chris said. "It didn't match the other art deco crap he's got going on in the hotel. We have to do something to entice people. Hopping, for those of us that have crossed over, is the best alternative to... blood. It gives the same rush without the consequences. That's what separates the Curioso from the Creeper."

"Why are you telling me this?" Vic asked. "Last I checked, my flesh and blood are still intact. Am I next in line?"

Chris shook his head. "Have you not listened to a thing I've said? Not anymore, Vic. You're nothing more than a glowing apparition with a dash of free will."

CHAPTER TWENTY-FOUR

NANCY HELBENS checked her leather watch. The nighttime shift was nowhere near its end. The lobby television remained a distraction that was more an annoyance than anything else. The spinning box fans in the corners hummed loudly, their unending drone merciless. Reaching into her jacket pocket for her lighter, she remembered the folded-up envelope the guest had left her that was also tucked in there.

I completely blanked out on this the other night.

Opening the letter with care, she studied the sloppy penmanship.

DANGER LURKS. Call me, and we'll chat some time. – Livewire, 555-5454.

She folded it up, placed it inside the envelope, and tucked it back into her pocket. She rubbed her eyes and began to yawn.

Well, that was useless. Good grief. I'm exhausted, she thought. *I can't keep covering both shifts like this. It's not good for me... or for Randy. The extra cash is nice, but the headaches that go with it are not. It's time for Greenwich to get that replacement hired!*

Part of normal morning checks included a courtesy call to guests on an extended stay. She dialed to room six-o-five since the eccentric arriver had not come back through the lobby since his arrival. The line trilled a few times, but there was never an answer.

Her mind fired on all cylinders.

Is today the day? The day I'm going to discover a suicide? A heart attack? A cocktail of medicines crisscrossed just the wrong way? I'm thinking too morbid. If there's one thing I'm being taught while working here, it's that nothing is definite or certain and that rules will be bent and broken. Let's have a look at the hotel policy manual and see what's written there.

Pulling out the aged volume Greenwich left beneath the desk, she blew dust bunnies from its top. The pages were thick but weathered in a leather-bound text, possessing an eerie texture that seemed unphased despite the hotel's previous inferno.

Nancy thumbed through the policy manual, finding the page dedicated to dealing with these kinds of situations. The rules were written in cursive, antiquated ink.

ON GUESTS WHO HAVEN'T CHECKED OUT

Always assume the worst. Death is more common in this business than most realize. Brace yourself for the grisly in hopes for something less.

She flicked through the pages of the book, shut it, and sneezed.

I guess I'll go on up there and check on him. Not the first guy I want to be in close quarters with.

She boarded the elevator, riding up to the sixth floor.

There's nothing to be afraid of, Nancy. This place protects you, remember? A hedge of protection like you've never known. I don't want to do this. No amount of overtime is worth it.

She walked the corridor of the floor, each step in a syncopated rhythm, and indicating her growing reluctance.

As she came to the southeast corner near six-o-five, the patterns and textures on the carpets jumped out at her, disorienting her as she fell to the floor, reliving the waking nightmare of her childhood.

***

Her parents continued their heated discussion as she peered around the corner. The fire burned as winter neared its pinnacle. Her mother, Bobbie, sipped spiked lemonade, while her father, Mitch, glared toward the woman in frustration — words having not been uttered between them in several minutes. Nancy stepped on a floorboard and it squeaked.

"What was that?" he asked, his defenses high.

"Just the house shifting," Bobbie said. "It's nothing."

Mitch sighed. "When are we going to talk about the Ouija board I found in the basement...? And that pagan book of spells!" he yelled. "You are getting mixed up with stuff our God never intended you to."

"It's just a way of life, Mitch," she said calmly. "I ain't hurting you... I ain't hurting her."

"Well, why don't you talk me through those sores on her arms? The sobbing I hear in the middle of the night. I swear if you've laid a finger..."

"You don't understand the female body and mind. She's just going through pre-pubescence like any girl her age would."

He flicked through their bank book. "It's more complicated than that. It's all of it combined — the tantrums, the unspoken anger, all of it festering when we least expect it. I swear you've cursed us all with your little club. What the heck are you ladies doing downstairs when we're not around? I've found rose petals, candles, wine bottles, goat bones. God knows what else."

"We're just exploring the earth around us. You know, finding our inner purposes," she said. "There's not a thing wrong with that."

Nancy crawled closer toward her parents, staying out of their line of sight.

"How does this fit into God's plan for us?" he asked.

She finished her drink. "If God created me and gave me free will, then *my* plan is what really matters. I know I'll answer for it one of these days. Until then, 'Eat, drink, and be merry, for tomorrow we will surely die.' It's in the Bible, right?"

"That's smart, but you're missing the point. You are misguided, Bobbie. I can't force you to do what you don't want to."

"You sure can't. And for that reason, I am very thankful. What *point* am I missing?"

"All this mystical, ethereal crap you're into has me concerned. What kind of garbage are you pumping into our kid's mind when I'm out making sales?"

"You won't have to worry about that, Mitch. You'll be getting papers soon."

"I should have known there was something off about you," he said, his eyes growing teary. "You were always poking the bear when I wasn't looking."

"Then, get your ass out," she yelled. "I'm serving you papers, Bible boy." She hurled a ball of yarn at him.

Nancy sniffled loud enough to be noticed.

"Who's back there?" Bobbie asked, hobbling across the room around the corner.

Nancy snuck back into her bedroom before her mother could spot her.

"Hmm. I must be hearing things," she said.

"On what grounds can you do that?" Mitch asked. "I've done nothing but treat you good."

"You've done nothing, alright! Irreconcilable differences. I'll leave you to the sofa for one more week and you can pack your crap up and get out."

Mitch stood up as tears continued trickling down the sides of his face. "I never saw this coming. I can't imagine how dark your soul must be."

Her grin was sinister. "Darker than you can ever know."

***

Nancy returned from her troubled memory, frustrated and wondering what mystical force or faction may have triggered it.

Alright, then. Six-o-five. Six-o-five.

Pacing toward the door, she took a breath before tapping on it.

"Hello, sir. It's Nancy from the concierge. We just wanted to perform a courtesy check. We hadn't seen you come through the lobby in a couple of days."

There was only silence.

What was it that made the other man snap in here? Thank God I wasn't the one to find him!

She knocked again, this time with greater firmness — the hollow echo reassuring her no one would come to open the door.

"Sir," she said, breathing deeply and projecting. "I'll be opening the door in two minutes if I don't hear from you."

I'm not ready to see a dead body... Maybe he won't be dead. He's just taken an extra sleeping pill and needs some extra prodding. What do I do?

Time ticked on with no one coming to answer room six-o-five. She pulled out the master key. Breathing in with care, she opened the aged mahogany door and stepped inside. Ramsey's bag sat on the disheveled bed. The television played another advertisement for clean water in third world countries.

Man, these infomercials are on nonstop.

The wall creaked, and the pit of Nancy's stomach bottomed out as she approached the darkened lavatory.

What was that?

There was only the faint red glow of the hotel's sprinkler system light flickering as she entered the room. She flicked the light switch on and it remained dark as the door closed behind her — her reddened reflection staring back in the mirror. She stepped toward the door, popping it back open, and wedging one of her shoes beneath to keep it from closing again. Her eyes adjusted to the dimness. Another figure appeared to lurk just behind the shower curtain. Faint whispers filled the air. She flicked the switch off and on again, and the light came on.

"Shit electrical," she mumbled, kicking the lavatory wall.

Pulling back the shower curtain, she saw remnants of black oil surrounding the drain. More of it dripped slowly from the shower head. She maneuvered toward the towel on the floor and picked it up. The flesh toned color on the towel breathed trouble.

Either this guy's got some bad bronzer, or there's something else off about this entire situation. I'll notify Greenwich.

She fumbled her way around the room and found Ramsey's notepad, taking it with her into the hallway and reading it as she climbed on the elevator.

CHAPTER TWENTY-FIVE

VIC RAMSEY and Chris Wilkerson sat close to one another. Their feet were propped against barrels stored in the halls. Despite the lack of solidarity between them initially, the bond that formed from hopping glued them together. Vic studied Chris and his eyes as they glowed.

"Why do your eyes... do that?"

"Appetite," Chris said.

"You said you don't need to eat anymore..."

"That's right, but I told you I have to feed my Curioso cravings. I feed them through hopping. The glow, and the appetite isn't there until you're reborn, though."

"What does that mean?"

"Those reborn outside their own skin don't have to feed their cravings, so their eyes don't glow. They aren't dead. Their second existence is just that, a second existence."

"Okay... I guess I get it, then."

"The fifth skeleton is tough to handle," Chris said. "You may not be ready."

"What's there for me to be concerned about?"

"This iteration is being replaced."

"What do you mean, iteration? I don't follow."

"He failed, and he's gone now." Chris said.

Vic shook his head. "I'm confused. You said there were six, right? There are five skeletons. It made the most sense to me that he would be the one that's missing. If he failed, shouldn't his skeleton be missing?"

"You're jumping to conclusions. I said I wasn't ready for the sixth seat to be filled... yet," Chris said, biting his lip. "Number five fell so far and so hard, he came totally undone. Worst part was, I'm sorry to say our reunion was news to me."

"Reunion? Who is he?"

"Yeah. Creeper Joe. You saw him when you hopped with me before. Some of our souls were linked to other bodies when the Shadow brought us back. Creeper Joe's never was. The Shadow told me that the skeletons must always remain in Oak Hollow for the unworthy to linger."

Vic ran his thumbnail between his front teeth. "Really?"

"This existence leaves me pondering. I get memories from time to time. I can't explain them. They're not always mine. I see faces and time periods I never lived in — far more primitive times than I grew up in. It's enough to leave a grown man shivering in his boots. I'll tell you that much. I never had those feelings before... before my change."

"What change?"

"You saw my vision, the moment the Shadow... that Wassermann brought me back," Chris said, hesitating a second. "Best I got it figured, the bones represent a piece of the soul my body was linked and resurrected with. Don't get me wrong. There are still parts of Chris Wilkerson that are definitely the man I once was, but I'm willing to admit that I've still got facets of myself now that I don't get, and I probably never will. Back to Joe..."

"Yeah, yeah." Vic nodded his head. "Who was he?"

"He was the failed protector of the tunnel,"

"Why would the tunnel need a protector?"

Chris bit his lip. "The Shadow expected him to protect the spring from the unworthy."

"The spring? Why? How did he do?"

"You'll just have to see for yourself. Let's hop. Grab hold of that fourth rib."

***

I can still hear them. Their neighboring voices screaming in misery as I slashed through their throats, running across the ballroom. Accountability at such an age seemed unfair, but I got what I deserved. In my retreat from it all, I ran into the tunnel where the men worked. Hoping to normalize my inner turmoil, I walked toward them to speak, and that's when I saw the Chipequan man light the dynamite. I had no time to react before the blast took us away in a moment's time. I laid there in the fire as life melted away, regretting the fifty-four I'd robbed from existence. She stood there, watching us all burn as if it were an acceptable thing to do. Our flesh burned away as the temperatures increased. I remember it all fading away.

I can't fathom why I was spared. It was an unspeakable mercy I never deserved. My first recollection in this existence was the Shadow hoisting me out of the spring, bringing me back up through it, and showing me my dripping bones.

"In this existence," he said, "you won't need them anymore. They're only a relic."

He dropped my bones into a black bag full of others and it fell to the floor. I saw him detaching another skeleton whose hand was attached to the bag. I assume the woman who watched us die must have drowned herself in the spring with the weight of our bones, carrying some unspeakable burden. The one thing I'm convinced of, we were all linked in that moment. The Shadow took me to the far end of the tunnel. And we bonded each of them together again – one piece at a time and into complete skeletons — few words ever being exchanged. It took more time than I want to admit and a few change-ups along the way, though. I struggled to fathom how the bones survived the blast as well as they did. The roots protected them, somehow padding the blow. Some got a second chance; others were transplanted into the lifeless body of another. That's how he distinguished us, the X's from the O's. He marked me with an X. I was the first to be reborn in my own skin. It didn't take long before I realized the conditions of this miserable... half-existence were worse than I could have fathomed. Listen to me rambling. I won't wander any longer.

Here I am years later, my eyes burning with fury as I drop the brass syringe to the floor to mask my inner agony. My recurring night terrors leave me wallowing in a restless hell. Far from fiction and further from fantasy, the Shadow forces me to relive my worst memories and traumas to pay my penance with the promise I'll one day be free again. The burning flames of my demise cover and scorch my wary mind. The tops of them dancing back and forth as the orange and the blue fade one into the other. That's when I see the woman in the tunnel drinking from the spring as if it were her own — the same one who watched us die. We never made eye contact, and it was probably for the better. I knew then and there; it would never be healthy for us to coexist. I must escape the recesses of this weary mind!

The Shadow jars me as he throws me into the past to relive one of my worst childhood memories. "This is the sin you pay for now, Joe. Watch it over again and suffer."

Pinning Debra Olsen's kitten in the corner behind their home, I teased her. "Cats are meaningless. Let's rid the world of this pointless thing."

Debra started to cry as she spoke, "Joey, don't do that. My daddy gave her to me. You know how much she means to me."

I grinned at her like a fool, speaking with the authority an overconfident teenager might be expected to have. "Exactly. You shouldn't be bowing down to any idols, girl. You 'worship' her. Look at how much attention you give her every single day. You're not her mother. What good are mothers, anyway? You wouldn't know. Would you? Your momma's out messing around with every guy in town but your old man... just like mine. What kind of person does that to their child? To their husband? The despicable and deplorable kind. Here I am just trying to teach you the hardest lessons in life. You'll have to learn them at some point, anyhow. God gives, and He takes away."

Debra choked back her tears, somehow still finding the words. "No. God isn't doing this, Joey. You are. You can stop this. You don't have to do this."

I grin at her something awful, knowing I have a terrifying look in my eyes. "You know I do, Deb. Reverend Selsky says it's my job to keep the kids in this area in check. *I'm* no saint, but *you* are definitely a sinner."

I grabbed the small kitten, torturing it arduously before stringing it up from the magnolia tree in the Olsen's backyard. Debra cried before slapping me in the face and running inside.

A moment later, she opened the door, squalling at me, "I'm going to tell my daddy on you, Joey. You're going to pay for this. I'll make sure of it!"

I laughed loudly in my uneven moment and said, "I hope it costs more than your momma makes messin' around every night, girl. She's a looker, after all. Heh-heh."

I continued to loiter, playing in the front yard until Debra's father, David Olsen, arrived home, waving at me as he entered. Moments later, he returned to scold me.

"Son, do you have any idea what you have done to my girl? You scarred her for life... You know it? Freak!"

He smacked me with his clenched left fist, bruising my shoulder on impact.

"She can't unsee what you did to her. I don't know what your momma and daddy are going to do with you, son. You're just... what... fourteen?"

I responded sheepishly, "Fifteen, sir."

"Well, for starters, go pick on your own kind, idiot. Leave my child and our pets alone, home wrecker. When your pop gets home, you send him over to my house. I don't want to have to come back over here myself. You hear me?!"

The memory ends, and I speak to the Shadow, "I know there are consequences. I lost my way teasing her that day. It was wrong to savor the taste of a debauched justice. Maybe it was hormones... or the unforgotten abuse of my parents, the absence of their love. Little Debra never deserved that, though. A mind warped that young is a mind forever torn away from its real potential."

The Shadow pats me on the shoulder. "I'm glad to see you're coming to grips with the unfortunate truth. That's been my hope for you all along."

Tormenting voices whisper in my head, one after another. I'm convinced it's the fifty-four I've slain. *Forever trapped. You damned fool. You never listened, and you'll never leave.*

***

"Dear God in heaven," Vic said, returning from the hop with Wilkerson. "You were right. I never want to see that again. What a miserable existence. He was like... *us?*"

"Joe's been purged from our lore. We shouldn't speak about him."

"Lore? This world is as real as anything else. Isn't it?"

"Of course it is," Chris said. "I just mean that the five of us can no longer be the original six we once were, and I think that went against the Shadow's plan to restore us. Greater answers lie somewhere deep in the recesses of our minds. I can see it in some of the hops. It's just fractured fragments I have to recall. Falling away like Joe did is not something to allow our minds to gravitate to for extended periods. Second chances only happen in fairy tales."

"Wait, this existence sounds like a second chance to me."

"It's complicated," Chris said. "It's more like a chance to finish the first. We were robbed, because *they* were robbed."

CHAPTER TWENTY-SIX

Wilkerson stared at the ceiling as VIC RAMSEY processed the things seen with each hop. The dark corridor on the eastern wing of the hotel seemed a peculiar hideaway without a definitive purpose. Their stationary and immobile state seemed almost vegetative until the clock struck two.

Wilkerson grew animated, and Vic spoke, "It's my turn to hop in someone other than one of these skeletons. No one in their right mind should be up at this ungodly hour."

Wilkerson shook his head. "Think that through for a moment. Do you want to hop into the head of someone not in their right mind?"

"It's just a figure of speech. He might be from another part of the world—you know, not adjusted to the time difference."

Moving toward an illuminated window, Vic started trying to force it open.

"Wait a minute," Wilkerson said. "We're hopping between the skeletons. You're not ready to hop into a living human yet... seeing through a guest's eyes, I mean. It's a much bigger burden because we have no control if they detect us mining their brains. Trust me."

"I can handle it. I've already had a taste of Creeper Joe. How much worse could it get?"

"Much worse! For all we know, the man just yanked a woman from the lobby, threw her into the bathtub, and shocked her with the hairdryer."

"I'd rather not entertain such sinister thoughts," Vic said.

"What's your hurry, anyway? We've already been over this. This shadowy sub-existence is hard to define, let alone grasp."

Vic breathed through his nose and sighed. "I think you need to show me more about *your* discoveries, then."

"I've got no qualms with that. Return to the third skeleton."

***

The tunnel remains dark. I'm unsure where the others have gone. Their faces are all washed out in my memory, hazy and out of focus, like something seen in the worst of nightmares. Studying my reflection in the uncommon water, an unfamiliar face stares back – thick, dark hair, my eyes black as night, and golden-brown skin that points back to the native origins of another.

The Shadow emerges. "Hello, Chris."

He pitches his top hat onto the spring where it floats in the center and spins. My eyes are drawn to it, but I know it will lead me to a place I don't want to go.

"You don't have to..." he says.

"I said nothing."

"I know. I just sense it." He moves closer toward me. "The free will of your kind is no different from the free will of a man."

"Why so ambiguous?" I ask.

"That's the name of the game," he says.

"What game?"

"Life. Death. Rinse. Repeat. It's your afterlife."

"No heaven or hell?" I ask.

He pulls out a cigar, lighting it and puffing it into the air. "There is. You're just stuck in between."

"You say that quite casually," I mumble, pointing to his face. "I see the mutton chops are still razor tight."

"Yes, they are. You're all stuck. All five... six... of you."

"Five or six? What do you mean?"

"A figure of this kind emerges once every nine years," the Shadow says. "You're number six. Joe's crossed over. There's only five of you left now."

"I don't understand," I say, pointing to myself. "Why me?"

"You're all connected."

"How's that?" I ask him, pointing to his cigar.

"Creepers are half of the equation. You're at a fork in the road, Chris. You can choose to be a Creeper, or you can take the higher road like others have chosen."

"What are you?"

"That's irrelevant," he mutters, puffing on his cigar.

"Care to elaborate?" I say, mystified by the entire situation.

"You're just awakening. Two Creepers, Two Curiosos, and one Undecided. You can remain an Undecided for one interval. Most choose their destiny well before that."

"To what end?" I ask. "What do I have to gain? Everything doesn't have to be black or white, does it? I like the gray area. That's where I belong."

CHAPTER TWENTY-SEVEN

NANCY HELBENS arrived in the lobby after collecting what was left of Ramsey's belongings. The husky voice of a woman came from a distance.

"Nancy Helbens, I need to see you now," she called out.

Who's in the basement? It sounds like... her. What do you want? Only imagination, Nancy. There's no one there.

"Get your rotund behind down here before I make you eat sand," the voice yelled.

It's not possible. I'll just respond to quiet my mind.

Nancy looked at the empty lobby. "I've got to tend to a customer. I can't. I'm sorry."

"There's no one else in the lobby," she yelled. "That lying tongue of yours will get you into heaps of trouble. Speaking of heaps... how about you come to me and I'll heap some burning coals on you? I'll have you know a medium-rare yields a better return. My first fifteen paintings are *living* proof of that. Ha-ha. I'll be the first to remind you... you owe me... remember? You owe me twofold, now!"

"I don't think so. You can come talk it over with me up here."

"I can't violate my lease. I'm not authorized to enter the hotel above ground."

"Well... I guess that's the end of this discussion, then."

"Not at all," the voice yelled, scratching her lengthy fingernails on the wall below. "One way or another, I'll be back for you. We've got to get squared up."

Nancy sat at the front desk. Fidgeting with every object in reaching distance, she remained restless. She returned to the trauma as her imagination failed to slow the terrors — her mother's eccentric behaviors growing more and more peculiar with time.

Swirling the sparkling wine in her glass, Bobbie Helbens sipped rapidly, leading Nancy to the nearly barkless live oak in the backyard. She patted the tree.

"Such a smooth surface. There ain't nothing like a good Chardonnay. Mmm. Mmm." She poked Nancy in the ribs. "Don't you be a drunk now like your father. He was worthless, Nancy. Worthless... Worthless... Worthless..."

"Dad never drank."

"Whatever," Bobbie said, swirling the wine in her glass. "He was so convinced working a nine to five was enough. A stupid Bible salesman going door to door. Who knows what he would do to sell those things to the bimbos sitting at home in their cozy evening wear all day long waiting for him to knock? He never knew how to treat me like a woman. Never. That wasn't what bugged me. He and I had our moments, but more often than not, he just went into his tiny office and wrote names, addresses, and sales. Names... addresses... and sales. What a boring, simple little man. I'd be lying if I didn't admit he charmed me the first night he came to my door. Your Uncle Herb and I were still rooming together well into our twenties." She slurred her words. "Anytime your father set me off, I'd come back here, and peel off layer after layer of the bark on his precious live oak. Nothing made him angrier. I like to break skin when I bite, Nancy. Sink some venom in while I'm at it. I'd act like it was all smoothed over and ease up on him a few hours before bed, maybe even get flirty. Then, when he'd fall asleep, I'd shove pieces of the bark in the back of his throat. You remember how superstitious he could be? The dumbass was never any wiser to know I was screwing with him. I'd tell him he was hexed. He'd go to the morning mass and do his Hail Mary's like clockwork... every single time."

She reached up toward her eye level, finding one of the few pieces of bark that lingered. Lunging toward Nancy, she lit up a match — its flame catching hold on the harvested wood. She scraped the bark up and down the sides of Nancy's arms. "To heal your dirty skin, my child." She pulled off another piece. "This one's to clean out your overstuffed loins. Break it into pieces."

Nancy tried to push her mother away as Bobbie kept scraping the bark all over her. Shoving the bark into Nancy's mouth, she grabbed her by the jaw and held it closed. "Chomp it up," she yelled. "It'll clean out your innards. It might even drop you a pant size."

Tears welled up in Nancy's eyes as her mother bullied her into submission. She ran further and further away in those moments, imagining anywhere and everywhere else she would rather be. Her father had been a source of joy and pleasure in her life, but Bobbie desperately wanted to deprive her of that in every way possible, deluding her with false memories and mountains of misdirection to make herself look better.

CHAPTER TWENTY-EIGHT

VIC RAMSEY sat in the lawn chair next to Wilkerson. The dark red glow of the space left the pair only faintly illuminated. Sitting in a transcendental trance of sorts, they studied the cinder blocks and large barrels that lined the walls. Wilkerson grabbed Vic by the arm, but neither could vocalize anything in the unpredictable moment. His mind remained stationary as he sat still in a willful effort to remain peaceful and calm.

"Chris, where do we go when it's not our... time?"

"It's all black, Vic. Darkness and screams. Memories and misfired imaginations. You start to see hell. You know, just get a taste of it."

"I don't know that I'm there yet, then."

"Good."

"I know you've seen it. Jump into the fourth skeleton. You'll see it all."

***

There she is. That old witch... I wonder how many decades she's been teaching this class. Probably longer than this building's existed.

I hear her awful voice as it ekes out each word, "Class, I'll be setting up an art club for those that wish to dig deeper in the less conventional methods of real art. For those interested, please meet me after school in the library."

The bell rang. Ms. Agatha Haney waved us all away. I turn in my paper, noticing my nicely printed name, Mary Cathel, in the top right corner. Mary Cathel—Ms. Haney's most prized student. The pride of West Riverton High. She doesn't make eye contact with me or even bother with any other acknowledgement. There's a knot in the pit of my stomach telling me not to go to the library, but I can't seem to resist. I loiter near my locker for a few minutes and then head that way. I have to know if this lady is a witch or if my sixteen-year-old mind is just filled with swirls of delusions. Ms. Haney's just... different. I'm walking into the library and there's not a soul in there except her. She has a defeated look in her eye as if she's done something terribly wrong and everyone but her knows it. I feel sorry for her. Ms. Haney studies me a moment. "Well, I guess it's just us," she says. "Shall we?" She motions toward the exit.

"Where are we headed?" I ask.

"Oh, I have a place where I find all inspiration for my art," she says, her eyes aglow. "I've been going there since I was your age. It changed my life."

"Where's that?"

"It's hard to describe," she replies. There's something strange about the way she answers. The tone in her voice. "Just come with me," she says, her uncommon smile hinting at a storied past.

I ponder on an audible to get out. "I should let my parents know."

"I wouldn't sweat it," she says. "I'm a teacher. They won't mind. The Riverton School District and all the taxpayers have faith in me to take care of you."

Not really... you're just a substitute that's overstayed your welcome. [My thought, never something I'm brave enough to say.]

"Okay, then," I reply. "Let's make it quick. My mom was supposed to pick me up at Corner Brothers at six. Will that work?"

"We'll get you back by then. Don't worry," Agatha says, smiling back at me.

She doesn't say much else as we continue to walk. I realize about halfway to our destination that we could have driven there unless Ms. Haney doesn't have her license or she doesn't want her location to be known. I break up the silence as we trek across town.

"I saw what you've been doing," I say, trying to keep the conversation interesting.

"What did you see, child?"

"Circling the letters on the board the last few weeks. Three letters per day. You've been sending a subliminal message, haven't you?"

She smiles toward me, her filed teeth sharper than I recall. "All of us brilliant ones figure out a way to communicate to others of matching mental caliber. I'm glad to see that you are attentive enough to pick up on that."

"Well, what's it mean?" I ask.

"Since you've been taking notes... Why don't *you* tell me what the message said?"

I pull out the sheet of paper from my pocket and hand it to her.

TO THE ASTUTE OBSERVER, MY NAME IS AGATHA HANEY. FOLLOW THE WITCH TO FIND YOUR PURPOSE.

"Seventy-two characters..." I call out. "You've been doing this for twenty-four school days."

"You're quite the savant, Mary. I could use more students like you participating in class."

I have to agree. This witch's intelligence and intrigue are growing on me. We get near a ground cover behind an abandoned building. I don't know if it leads to a sewer or what? She lifts it up and starts climbing in. I feel like something terrible is going to happen, but I follow her anyway. We're clanking down the steps. It's a bigger drop to the floor than I realize, and Agatha charges toward a spring fed area.

"Come on! Hurry, Mary," she yells, her voice echoing through the tunnel.

I make my way over and it's at this point I know that something's gone terribly wrong. She jumps into the spring and her face rejuvenates, regenerating her into a much younger and more vital woman than the one I recall seeing under the fluorescents West Riverton High. She takes a drink from it.

"This place is my escape, Mary. The path to my youth!" Her eyes are glowing brighter than I've ever seen — almost inhuman. "Our escape now, my child. Drink up. It'll show you things you could never imagine."

I swallow the drink and I pass on into some other existence like one I've never seen. Suddenly, I'm floating above town, and I see the old building we went behind to enter this vast tunnel. The place is a beautiful hotel, vital and thriving— bursting at the seams with people and opportunity. A young man walks in the building with a pronounced hobble, and that's when lightning seems to strike. Not literally, but in my vision. Coming back to my senses, I soak in the spring, realizing how drenched my clothes are and pondering what my mother will think if I ever get home and try to explain what happened. A figure hovers above me. He reaches in to pull me out, and that's when Agatha screams.

"Get out!" she yells. "I already warned you... and you still don't get it, do you?"

There's no reply. He hobbles away, drifting into a dark corner.

There are six skeletons sitting on stones, and remnants of ash in an old firepit.

Agatha chants into the air, holding a piece of my hair as she grabs the rib of the fourth skeleton. She speaks incoherently (or at least it seems that way) and I levitate into the air. I don't know what's happening, but I transcend everything at the top of the tunnel. She yells and I'm dropped into the dirt from the ceiling. Only minutes later, I awaken being pulled from the spring. Agatha has disappeared in the moment. Somehow, I'm still conscious despite my body's inner workings struggling to operate. It feels different, though. I'm now carrying emotions and memories that certainly aren't my own. I'm finally free to escape this temporary taste of hell. Yes, something's definitely changed. I just can't grasp what. A shadowy figure nods his head toward me, quickly leaving me after my... rebirthing. Then I see Agatha again. She removes her red-framed glasses as they dangle from the chain, an unquenched sweat pouring down her cheeks. Her knitted sweater sings a far less sinister song than she's truly capable of, and I know this now. She speaks to the air, either to another being I cannot see or just manically to herself.

"Intelligence is fleeting," she says. "It's not worth the hassle."

She chants incantations as her body trembles, the earth shaking beneath her. I lay on the ground motionless. Her eyes turn scarlet red as her body lifts. Is she some kind of priestess? A witch? Or just a poser weirdo I'm on an acid trip with? Who knows? The skeletons rise around her, encircling her and spinning her faster and faster in the air until she's thrown to the floor.

The shadowy figure that hoisted me out earlier comes back. And it's in that moment that Agatha falls prostrate to the floor and a hazy smoke overtakes the room.

"I can't rightfully pass the torch to you, Agatha," the figure says. "You should know the rules by now. A rule by a Creeper must always be followed by rule of a Curioso. The balance of power through the years keeps this place vital, and it has for many years. You may stand and face me."

She rises in unspeakable reverence, looking at the floor as the figure glows behind the smoke.

"Do you care to elaborate?" she asks.

He speaks, "There is no need. I won't be trapped by duplicity. There's no conjuring your way to the top, so don't bother trying."

"What are you, Wasserman? A caretaker?" she asks, stepping closer toward him. He puts his arm around her, pulling her close.

"Caretaker's too weak. I'm more like a master of ceremonies," he says, somber in the moment.

"You're so stoic when you speak..." she says. "I think you probably always were."

"That's the best way..." he replies, "and it should be the only way. A path to diplomacy."

"Diplomacy? I was thinking more along the lines of you having a good poker face," she says.

Agatha's eyes are narrow, her face scarred from a distant past, and yet, the lingering embrace from the figure called Wasserman seems sincere — father-like in a way. She looks over Wasserman's shoulder as she hugs him tighter and tighter, and stares into my eyes as the amber in her own becomes more prominent.

"I want to know you more, Will..." she says, "to know your inner most thoughts. What will that take?"

"It won't take," he replies with great confidence. "It's not an option."

Her smile grows sinister, rivaling that of the finest of villains.

"I guess we're at a bit of an impasse, then," she says.

***

Vic returned from the hop.

"What do you think?" Chris asked.

"This Mary Cathel... Is she dead?"

"I've never met her," Chris said. "I couldn't say."

"I'm not sure what to make of the rest..."

"Well, these glimpses are not by chance. Not a single one of them. What's revealed is what he feels are pertinent."

"He?"

"Yes. You should know by now... the Shadow," Chris said.

CHAPTER TWENTY-NINE

Placing the RING BELL FOR SERVICE placard on the front desk, NANCY HELBENS made her way into the basement to check on Randy during her lunch break. [His bedtime had been three hours earlier, but her work hours left her unable to check on him often.]

The television in the lower level sitting room played her *NightWatch* interview.

Why is this on? Look at that chunky face. It won't hurt to leave Randy alone a bit longer. How stupid was I to go on national TV and flap my jaws like that? she thought.

"Yeah, it was a terrifying experience." She looked away in hesitation. "The creep owned the horror hotline, inflicting punishment on each one of us like we were toys."

"Do you care to elaborate?" the host said theatrically. "I mean no offense, but what kinds of things did he do?"

She swallowed, looking away as the camera faded into her answer. "He stuffed rats and bats down our throats the few times he'd show his face and gag us when he finished. There were these sprinklers in the ceilings for fire emergencies, but instead of being linked to water lines, they were connected to tanks full of bleach. He'd just sit there and watch it burn our skin on the video cameras. It was never enough to kill us — but it was miserable. Look at my arm here. You can still see it." She held her arm out as the camera panned toward it, showing the bleach inflicted scar.

"Dear God…" the host said, his face flushing. "What do you think was going through his mind that day, Nancy? What can you share with the rest of America about your experience to prevent them from running into their own sadistic Creeper 'round the corner?"

"Buy a gun, watch your back, and avoid old buildings like the plague."

"Wise words from a scarred woman," the host said, his veneers obvious, and excessive plastic surgeries evident. "Thanks for your time, Nancy."

"I can't say it's my pleasure, but the truth had to come out. I'm just glad he's dead."

"They say the body went missing. Is that accurate?"

She hesitated. "Yeah. I've heard that."

"Wait, is there something you're not telling us?

Nancy shook her head. "Joe is a... a..."

"Joe? You've been telling us about Chris all along. Who's Joe?"

"I'm sorry. I had a moment of brain fog. I get this way occasionally when I'm nervous. Yes. It was Chris Wilkerson. I don't know where the name Joe came from," she said, laughing nervously.

"Nancy, we're out of time. It's been an honor." He stood up to shake her hand. "Thank you for your bravery to share this... unpalatable truth with us tonight."

She nodded her head on screen and the video cassette came to an abrupt stop.

Some kind of marketing for your hotel — friggin' Greenwich. Reliving my glory days? Spying on my televised cleavage?

She walked over to the television and turned it off before entering her barren apartment. Randy was not in bed as expected. Since the separation, she had made no extra effort in decorating the abode provided.

"Randy... are you in the bathroom, son?"

There was no reply.

"Randy, if you can hear me, call out to me! Are you okay?"

She started going around the compact room, turning over every pillow, looking behind the furniture, the other side of the shower curtain, and inside the lavatory cabinets. Randy was nowhere to be found. She shrieked. Facing the mirror, her eyes bottomed out as she saw herself swinging from a noose in the room's corner.

Pull yourself together, Nancy. It's all in your mind. That's all. This is a huge hotel. He could be anywhere... with anyone. Who knows what they're doing to him? I am a terrible mother, she thought.

Her heart pounded harder as she frantically searched through the basement. After pounding on Greenwich's door and receiving no reply, she forced her way into his office.

She gritted her teeth. "I swear Jerry Greenwich, if you laid a hand on my boy, I'll kill you."

Rifling through a few of his personal effects on the desk, she hoped for a clue.

There's got to be something... seriously... come on!

She ran to the aquamarine curtains, rushing toward them, and peered into the tunnel. Before she could look around any further, she saw Greenwich gagged and roasting over a fire like a charred rotisserie. Agatha was nowhere to be seen. Her eyes wandered a moment, studying the tunnel. The top eight levels of The Oak Hollow Hotel had indeed protected her from her past terrors, but nothing could eradicate the pain and emotional toll inflicted upon her by Creeper Joe. While beneath the surface (whether in the basement or the tunnel), she was vulnerable.

The friggin' cops won't even come anymore if I call. I'll just take matters in my own hands.

CHAPTER THIRTY

VIC RAMSEY studied the corridor. Wilkerson nodded toward the next skeleton.

"I hope this experience is enriching. These are big shoes to fill," Chris said.

"I guess we'll see."

Curtains from one of the neighboring windows were flung open.

"Don't move a muscle," Chris said. "He won't see you."

The guest attempted to force the window open but remained unable, pulling it abruptly closed.

"Alright," Chris said. "Let's go ahead. This one ought to intrigue you. If we see the event I've seen in my past hops, that is."

They moved toward the first skeleton, setting themselves up to hop. He grabbed the fifth rib.

***

I walk into the back of the Bridgewater Saloon as the frustrated owner's voice creaks, "Renzell, we don't want you or your kind lingering around in here. You can pick up your food in the back."

"Excuse me?" I say, staring him down, "My kind?"

"The Chipequa sold their stake in Oak Hollow to the Wasserman's fair and square," the man says. "There just ain't no way to be polite. Your traditions and earth lovin' ways are crampin' our style."

I clench my fist near my jaw tightly. "And how is that? We have just as much right to be here as anyone else, don't we?"

The man gawks at me, looking toward his enforcer to remove me from the premises. "And my momma ain't prejudiced. Get on out before I have to straighten out that enormous nose you've got on ya."

I squint my eyes toward the ugly yellow-toothed man, gritting my teeth together as I speak, "The Chipequa ancestors roll in their grave seeing your hatred."

The man spits on the ground toward me before wiping his chapped lips. "Well, tell them they ain't welcome here, either."

I get in touch with my roots, chanting and calling to my ancestors, the former Chipequa elders. "Icthe ireini voo, goola ona oba. Icthe ireini voo, goola ona oba."

"What in tarnation are you doin'?" the owner yells. "Toss him out of here, Ray!"

The room fills with smoke as the man is enveloped. As it clears, a pile of dust and ash remains beneath.

I look toward the man he called Ray and say, "Get a broom and sweep him out of here. Or, they'll teach you a lesson, too, buckaroo." I walk out of Bridgewater, an unsung hero overwhelmed by the unhinged injustices the Chipequa faced.

***

Chris looked toward Vic. "Steve's a successful businessman now — tame and wise beyond his years, and living proof that all men have great potential, all the while overcoming insurmountable odds and hatred. There is hope yet."

"Thanks for sharing that," Vic said, a kindred spirit in the moment. "I could never have known."

He looked toward Wilkerson. "I'm trying to piece it all together. This is a lot to take in. I have to admit though, I am fascinated."

CHAPTER THIRTY-ONE

NANCY HELBENS rushed across the basement, going into the closet inside Greenwich's office.

I bet she's got you again, Randy. I don't know where else you would have gone.

Jerry's suits and ties were on a rack covering the back wall. She pulled them aside to see the Cardinal Rules of the property etched on the cornerstone. Creeper Joe's echoing laugh raced through her mind.

Heh-heh!

Goodness' sake... she thought. *I hadn't seen these in ages.*

1. NEVER DISRESPECT THOSE THAT ARE LESSER. PUT THEM ON A PEDESTAL AS IF THEY WERE ROYALTY ANSWERING TO A HIGHER POWER. [DON'T LET YOUR EYES BE HAUGHTY. LOVE THEM LIKE THEY NEVER WERE.]
2. NEVER TALK ABOUT THE UNEXPLAINABLE THINGS THAT YOU SEE TO STRANGERS. IT WOULD BE TOO EASY TO BE A FALSE WITNESS.
3. DON'T STIR UP TROUBLE IN YOUR COMMUNITY.
4. NEVER SET FOOT WHERE YOU AREN'T WELCOME... YOUR FEET WILL BE QUICK TO RUSH TO EVIL.
5. DON'T RECYCLE ANYONE ELSE'S WORDS AS YOUR OWN. A LYING TONGUE ONLY LEADS TO TROUBLE.
6. NEVER SHED INNOCENT BLOOD.
7. NEVER HAVE A HEART THAT DEVISES WICKED SCHEMES.

Finding her way through, she nudged the wall, squeezing through a crack that led into the tunnel.

Should I call for him? Or will I end up roasting on the fire next to Greenwich?

She walked through the corridor as traumas from the past overtook her mind. Memories flashed in front of her like they were yesterday, Joe's unforgettable laugh continuing to echo through her mind, the scent of alcohol reeking from her mother as she berated her in her younger years, and Randy's distinct cry in his early months.

She grounded herself in those early moments with Randy. Moving within the shadows of the mostly empty and forgotten tunnel, Nancy studied it, even finding the alcove she called home from her time there. The homely person held captive in the tunnel was nothing like the woman and mother she had become after Randy's birth.

I'll sit for a bit and see if I can hear him, she thought. *No one knows him better than I do.*

Her reluctance to speak carried with it an inexplicable weight. The tormenting memories deflected across the shadows of Oak Hollow were loud while in the tunnel — and screaming at her full force. In this moment, her fight or flight was triggered. There was no stopping Nancy Helbens on her quest to recover Randy.

She tiptoed through the tunnel until she heard the crackle of a fire and soft-spoken voices in the corridor. Approaching quietly, she saw the back of Randy's overgrown red headed chili bowl facing a flesh toned canvas as his whistle echoed through the tunnel. He was painting.

Who's watching me? she thought. *I feel them.*

Nancy approached Randy. As she neared him, she whispered, "Son, we need to go."

"No, we don't, Nancy. I'm staying with my mommy."

"What? Randy, *I'm* your mother."

Agatha's voice cackled across the room. She walked out, sipping from a pewter cup. "Ha-ha-ha. I'm sorry to say it, but the late Nancy Helbens has been officially replaced by a mother more suitable. Come here, sweetheart. Mommy will hold you close."

Randy ran toward Agatha as she wrapped her arms around him. The glow in her eyes startled Nancy.

"You messed with the wrong mom on the wrong day, bitch!" Nancy said, with throatiness in her voice.

"Nancy... Nancy... Nancy... Your mother... was a pawn of epic proportions, wasn't she?"

"What are you saying?"

"She got mixed up," Agatha said.

"Give me my Randy back!"

Agatha patted him on the back. "Why should I? He's got all the love and affection he could ever need in a mother right here. Never a worry or a care in the world – and far from the endless blathering of societal pressures to create a thoughtless, voiceless child controlled by a relentless government machine."

She studied Agatha closely. "What are you talking about?"

"I know I may be on the fringes, honey – but I'm not stupid. We're all being brainwashed. The system is set up to help the prosperous prosper more and the poor suffer worse."

Nancy's voice escalated. "You are some kind of deluded. Randy, come on. She can't keep you anymore. This is your decision."

Agatha grinned at Nancy. "Why do you say that? I mean... you've got this old... 'bitch' curious."

"I've read the hotel policy manual back and forth. I don't know how Jerry could have been such a fool, trusting you with this space."

"I seduced him, Nancy. Men are weak in the knees when they're lonely. They're hungry for a desire that can't be satisfied. Do you follow?"

Nancy scoffed. "Unless you're going to hex *me* now, I've got nothing else to say to you."

"Mommy, I'm scared," Randy called out, looking at Nancy indecisively.

"It's okay, sweetheart. Mommy's here," Nancy said.

Randy scrunched his nose, shaking his head. "Not you. I'm talking to my *real* mommy."

Agatha cackled loudly, the echo resonating through the far reaches of the tunnel. "Oh, my sweet child, you don't have to worry anymore. Mommy will protect you from this liar." She patted Randy as he cuddled closer to her, glaring toward Nancy — her eyes aglow. "I'm going to ask you to leave, unless you have something else *meaningful* to contribute. You owe me, remember?"

Nancy sighed. "Fine... I'll pay up."

Agatha stroked her fingers through Randy's hair. "How might you do that?"

"How about settling an old score with a double-crossing sociopath?"

"That's enticing. Randy, go with Nancy for a while. Mommy will be waiting."

"I don't understand, mom. Why would you let me go with the liar?"

Agatha answered, her voice sweet and soft, "Nancy has to... settle a score with your mommy."

"What does that mean?"

"Give us a second." She covered Randy's ears. "Nancy, I agreed with your request to stage the kidnapping with Randy because you wanted a cop out to break it off with Ron. Lest you forget, dear child, our arrangement was conditional."

Nancy kicked dirt from the floor toward Agatha. "I don't see it that way, hag! Give me the kid back."

Agatha scoffed, putting her arm around Randy's shoulder. "Is that the most possessive you're going to get with this sweet boy? *The kid*?" Agatha said, doing quotation marks with her fingers.

"Don't get into an argument with me over semantics."

"Bring Bobbie here, and I'll leave you alone. Deal?" she uncovered Randy's ears and whispered to him.

He walked over to Nancy, looking back toward Agatha for approval.

"I'm not going to wheel and deal with a demented witch... I'll get her here. You can do what you want to with her." Nancy covered Randy's ears. "Line her up next to Greenwich! Turn her into a friggin' filet mignon for all I care! Whatever the hell you do with her is better than letting her continue to waste clean air on God's green earth."

Agatha laughed. "I'll be waiting. You don't have to bring her back here. I'll tell you what. Bring her sorry ass to your little smoking patio behind the hotel. We'll have us a real proper exchange."

Nancy nodded. "Okay, give me a few hours and I'll get her over here."

CHAPTER THIRTY-TWO

VIC RAMSEY stroked the sides of his unshaven cheeks as he pondered. He and Chris sat across from one another at a card table as the buzz and glow of the EXIT sign filled the dead air surrounding them.

I don't think I have a grasp on what's happening to me, he thought. *Will I ever?*

"Chris, how can we escape this existence?" he asked.

"You mean... end it?"

"Yeah."

"If I had a simple answer, I would have been trying to get to that point a while back."

"Maybe it *is* a simple answer," Vic said, standing up from the lawn chair. "Have you ever considered that you were overthinking it?"

"I don't think that's possible."

"Maybe that's why I'm here," Vic said, "to help you see."

"I guess anything's possible. Why don't you move toward the second skeleton and grab the right shoulder?"

Vid nodded. "Okay."

***

Agatha yells in a shrilling tone as I fall to the floor, deafened by her extravagant volume. I wait inside while she lures a group of followers into the tunnel. She looks at me. "My friend, Bobbie, still has a lot to learn about herself, too. Don't be afraid," she says, patting one of the other young ladies on the back as they follow her through the long, dark tunnel.

I already have the fire lit per her request.

"Everyone, come closer, around the fire," she says. "Grab each other's hand and repeat, 'icthe sabanis reglo sein'... six times."

"Agatha, this ritual, what's it going to do for us?" I ask.

"Prosper you and damn the rest."

"That's not what you told me before," I say.

"I'm kidding. It will protect you and your home from evil. If we don't take matters into our own hands, the children can never be watched over properly. Now repeat after me, 'icthe sabanis reglo sein'... six times."

The group chants, "Icthe sabanis reglo sein... icthe sabanis reglo sein..."

Approaching the sixth time, they each grab at their chests as if a piece of their heart is stripped away.

"Ichthe sabanis reglo sein."

The others fall to the floor as their hearts stop, their flesh melts away, and only their bones are left. She pitches them into the spring, one after the next. I remain unaffected. She glares at me and then moves toward the spring. I've already had my moment in here. I've never admitted it to her, though. She's bound to know.

"Take my offering. Take my offering. Feed my youth," she calls out toward the spring, throwing fresh bones in. She dips her head back into the water and I see her age erasing itself. *Amazing. If this woman is hoarding an elixir of youth, I want some, too.*

The Shadow approaches, calling out to her, "What was the point, Agatha? No one else needed to die."

"Rekindling and rebirth. I feel a positive energy coursing through," she says. "The modern woman has much she's up against... and her youth is fleeting. Why not have a competitive advantage? It's already served me well. And we both know what I mean. Ha-ha."

"Positive energy?" he replies, puffing on his cigar. "Bitterness can't be changed. It's manifested from Satan."

"And what do we do?" she says. "We throw it back at him!"

***

Vic looked back at Wilkerson, scratching his head. "What did I just see?"

" *We* saw Agatha Haney back in '63," Chris said.

"Who were they?"

"She manipulated them through a complex form of hypnosis..."

"Hypnosis doesn't work that way," Vic said. "I know better. Now, I know you're lying to me."

"It may not be that effective, but when it's partnered with other mystical elements, it certainly can. I'll show you."

***

"Icthe sabanis reglo sein," Vic mumbled as he remained hypnotized.

Chris stopped a metronome. "Vic, wake up. Don't repeat that phrase again. The priest prayed the evil out of the hotel, but it still lingers in the tunnel."

Vic's eyes opened slowly as he stared back at Chris. "What the heck did you do to me? What did you say?"

"Not much. You drifted away and started talking about New Orleans... something about a voodoo doll, that they hypnotized you to move out of town and forget."

"Really? I don't remember that."

"Remember, in this existence, it might not be your memory. I don't have a good read on you, yet."

"I feel so lost," Vic said, "overwhelmed, I mean."

"A better glimpse into Bobbie might help."

"I'm not sure I want to go back," Vic said.

"It may not be the most enjoyable thing, but putting the pieces together could be a catalyst to a greater purpose."

Vic rested his hand on the back of his neck. "I can speculate. You can speculate. Aha moments happen from time to time, but being shaken to the core has side effects. And that's what keeps happening to me with this."

"Just give it another go," Chris said. "Grab the left shoulder."

"Okay."

***

He's been gone a while. I buried him in the backyard. I sit out here often, wondering if she'll ever know. I got sick of her clinging so close while I'm the one slaving over the hot stove, washing all her clothes and hanging them on the line, bathing her like clockwork. Her daddy always got the spoils while I was stuck with the rest. The afternoon came just like one of the many others, and I just gave in to my flesh. That's what Agatha encouraged me to do over and over as she guided me on my journey to this... better existence. I was better off. He resented me for the time I spent with her, and the truth was — it made me feel good inside knowing it burned him the way it did. I never had romantic feelings for Agatha, nor she for me. It was just a mutual sort of affection that sisters share. We were never sisters in the flesh, though — only in spirit. I remember it like it was yesterday. I sat out here much like I am today. He chased me around the house after he caught me peeking in one of my spell books and confronted me. Something about a God follower not being able to practice this kind of magic... blah, blah, blah. So, I'm a pagan now. Sue me. I had been reading on ways to get rid of him. I idealized it in my mind for weeks. I wanted the confrontation to be just right. Just my way and in *my* control — that moment where the stars and the sun finally align. There wasn't much of a fight. I love reliving that moment when the last breath escapes his body. It's liberating and invigorating. I never wanted to kill anyone else, just him. I go over and over it like I am now, studying that barren live oak in the backyard. It's been a few weeks. I told Nancy he walked out on us once and for all for a harlot across town. She never wanted to buy that. I knew it was a fabrication, too—but control is my heroin, and I'll never give it up. There was that feeling, slipping through my arm in a rush as I shoved the bark down his throat — cutting off his air supply and asphyxiating him. I know I've got issues. It's okay, though, because Mitch did, too. I enforced the rules my own way, and I'm better off because of it now. I'm enjoying the chirp of the birds, the freshly cut green grass, and living in the moment as I sip on my adult lemonade and crochet a little. There she is... the obese child comes barreling out the door. She glares at me, and I can't stomach seeing her anymore. Look at her, she despises me. Momma can't ever give her *what* she needs, momma can't be *who* she needs, and worse than anything else, momma can't even meet her own damn needs. I'm falling apart. My Nancy gets more and more hideous with each passing day. What kind of mother am I thinking this way? I guess it's just the way it has to be. My unhealthy mind wanders a savage path, and I can only recall what makes the most sense in this moment. She waddles across the grass like she's got an extra backpack full of jello in her gut, and I call out to her. She ignores me and keeps playing. I struggle not to take offense. What forsaken child snubs their mother this way? It's only natural that mine would. All that the sweet child needs is a genuine mother's love. I study the child closer, the buzz of the alcohol, the blue sky, and the scorching sun owning me as I give in to my frustration. It's an afternoon like many others, and her very presence has pushed every button I have left. I know I'm the problem, but somehow, I rationalize my actions by twisting her into the mix to make her feel as bad as I do. Somewhere deep down, I know it's wrong, but I still lash out as she drops into the sandbox, "Walk like a crab, kid. We've got to burn some more calories. The damn sun sure ain't cooking them off your big behind."

CHAPTER THIRTY-THREE

Livewire sat in the hotel lobby chair waiting. Lost in thought over her difficult moment with Agatha, NANCY HELBENS opted not to address him, instead sitting down at the desk and straightening things up.

I still haven't called the cops about Greenwich. I guess a few hours more isn't going to hurt. I'd like to see mom squirm when she sees Agatha again.

Randy walked over toward the sitting area as the television played.

Livewire spoke loudly, "What's your name, son?"

"Randy."

"Randy, huh? That's nice. A good simple All-American sort of name. Perfect."

"I'm Livewire."

"Livewire?"

"Yeah. That's right. My real name's Bob, but that's boring. Right?"

"Yes, sir."

I guess I'll go see what he wants, she thought. *I wasn't expecting any conversations today. Sure as hell not with him.*

Approaching the seating area, she sat down across from him, crossing her legs, her well-fitted black dress and heels clear evidence of her effort to seem put together.

"Hello," he said.

She took a deep breath. "Hi. I wasn't expecting *you* anytime soon. I didn't think you cared much for this place."

"I don't, but I care about old friends... A good friend is hard to come by. A great friend is even harder."

"I don't understand," she said. "I don't think that I'm either of those things to you."

"Your boy needs that from you, too. I can see it in his eyes."

Randy's attention was diverted to the Looney Tunes episode on the television, remaining aloof to the conversation.

"I'm sorry. I don't see how this is any of your business."

"I don't guess that it is. I just felt a tug on the old heartstrings after seein' you the other day. I'm not expectin' anything more from you. Just to be friends."

"Ron and I are having problems, but I don't think I can give that to you right now. It wouldn't be proper. Randy needs a better example from his mother."

"I hardly think separated parents makes an ideal situation for a kid."

"It does when the parents are struggling to get along. Or when the husband is as..."

Livewire interrupted, "I don't want to hear anymore. Maybe it was a mistake coming over here."

"I don't mean to disappoint you. We're just at a different phase in our lives. Carrying new kinds of baggage and responsibilities."

"Well, *you* are." He scratched at his stomach. "I think I'm about the same. Truth is, Nancy, my granddad and this property have long been a repellent for me. He died here."

She frowned. "I don't think you've ever told me that."

"It's not the kind of thing you bring up in a casual conversation. I get a little squirrelly when I'm around here. I always have. Even way back when."

"Is it any different now?"

"I was hoping it would be," he said. "but I don't think so. Fresh paint and new carpets can't erase the wrongs of the past."

"You are a deeper thinker than I ever gave you credit for, Livewire. I'm sorry."

He smiled at her. "There's no need for you to be sorry. A new day will dawn. I can feel it. It's like my grandfather is screaming it in my ear. All will be well one day."

"I hope so."

He stood up, patting Randy on the head. "It's nice to meet you."

"You too," Randy said.

"I best be getting on my way," he mumbled, moving toward Nancy and leaning in to hug her. "I hope you and Ron can work it out. You're an alright gal, Nancy Helbens."

"Thanks."

Livewire moved toward the revolving entry door and exited the building. The lights flickered a moment as he walked out.

That was odd. Hmm...

"Who was that, Nancy?"

"Mommy. Not Nancy," she said, grabbing Randy on the shoulder. "He was an old friend. I've got to call grandma. Stay over here for a minute, will you?"

"Okay, lady."

"Randy, I've had it up to here with the name calling. You are to address your parents the correct way. I'm mommy to you. Daddy is daddy to you."

He ignored her.

Approaching the lobby telephone, she picked it up, dialing Bobbie Helbens. After several trills, the woman lifted the receiver but spoke no words.

Nancy gulped. "Mom, it's me. I know we... uh... we uh... got off on the wrong foot the other day. I need your help with Randy. Do you think you could swing by the hotel and chat for a bit? Maybe you can take him for an ice cream. I'll explain better when you get here."

Bobbie sighed.

"I don't blame you for not wanting to come by, but I hope your grandson is a good enough reason to put our differences aside."

"If that's an apology, I'm not sure I buy it, but I love Randy. I'll get dressed and be over in a few minutes. I'll meet you out front."

"Is it too much to ask for you to come inside?"

"Yeah. I don't feel welcome with you around," Bobbie said. "It's best that I don't."

"Alright, then. I'll be watching for you. Thanks, mom."

The line disconnected.

Gosh, I feel awful. Maybe I should reconsider this... her mind drifted back to the seared flesh, the manipulation, and the wine and spiked lemonade tirades. *On second thought...*

CHAPTER THIRTY-FOUR

VIC RAMSEY followed Chris Wilkerson down the darkened hallway. The walls put off steam as a repetitive puffing sound began.

Man, it's getting warm in here.

"What is that?" he asked.

"Years ago, they used this space as a sauna. It's still got the hook ups. Greenwich just never fully set it up again. I think they lined the back wall with a long bench."

"Really? Why the windows looking into the area?"

"I think there were plans for a pool. It was supposed to be linked. The other thing I'm told, this was originally the top floor. Finances fell through and Wasserman left the idea behind, instead opting to profit better by adding two more floors."

Vic sighed, grabbing at his chest as his breath elevated. "I feel claustrophobic and weak. What's going on?"

"Don't worry, you're still adapting. Follow me this way."

Approaching the purple INFORMATION CENTER sign, Chris moved toward it, removing a loose cinder block and pulled out a couple of lukewarm Flitz beers and a can of peanuts. "I know it's not much to offer, but it will probably tide you over for a bit."

"Just my luck," Vic said. "This stuff seems to be everywhere, but I've yet to see anyone actually enjoy it."

Chris put his hand on Vic's shoulder. "I didn't even bother telling you how long it's been stored," he said with a smug grin. "Try changing your outlook. Once we accept the difficult truths in front of us, it's easier to pivot. When it comes to this place, there's no denying that history repeats itself. I try to forget every single day I continue on in this peculiar existence, and yet, I'm reminded there must be a greater purpose to still being here. I've studied these glimpses over and over for years, trying to make sense of why. Parts of the tunnels beneath the hotel were ruined when that native fellow lit the dynamite, and generations later, we still feel it."

"What a sad reality."

Chris nodded. "He was trying to sabotage the hotel. You know, hoping to cave it in. I can't blame him, though. The Wasserman's screwed the Chipequa over. He never meant to kill the others. Suicide can be a generational thing, right? His father's tears seeped through him like they were his own, long after he was gone. I've relived it... many times over. I reckon he left a piece of himself with all the victims that day, born, reborn, and in between. We all see it, and it's quite haunting."

"Of course, and why wouldn't it be?"

Chris motioned toward the skeletons that surrounded. "It's imperative for you to understand this, because I don't think you understand. We remain under his care...Wasserman... The Shadow."

"What do you mean? Is he not one of us?"

"No. He's our guardian. You'll become more acquainted in due time. The struggle is, he's carrying a burden that he can't release."

"The hotel?" Vic asked, rubbing his chin.

"I don't think so. He's conflicted by conviction. He told me so himself. Forever a slave to Oak Hollow. Thing is, with that indebtedness comes unfathomable power. I don't envy him. I admire the heck out of him, though."

"That's it, Chris..." Vic said, without further hesitation. "That's why you're still here. Maybe even the reason for a lingering existence on these grounds. It's not common knowledge that the Chipequa's past has been purged from Riverton – It disappoints me to fathom the reasons, but it's not too late to make it right."

Chris looked away from Vic. "You know something. You may be right. I'm embarrassed to admit I overlooked something so simple."

Vic's eyes narrowed as he spoke, "I don't mean to treat you as asinine, but I think that's it. It's no cliché. It truly is unfinished business. These grounds aren't cursed because of who is buried beneath. They're cursed because of what was never buried above." He nodded his head, moving closer toward Chris. "Sometimes, the lessons we learn the slowest are the ones whose answers lie the closest."

Chris blinked rapidly. "The Shadow's shown it to me for years, and I've just missed it."

"I'd wager he's the lynchpin to the problem."

"Maybe. He passed away right here in Oak Hollow, October 29th, 1910, — he's been hanging around ever since. Or, so he's told me."

"Okay. And, what of Agatha?"

"About Agatha," Chris said, "she deludes you until you can no longer distinguish your inherited memories from your actual realities. It's a psychological and emotional manipulation she's evolved with pagan and mystical roots."

"Has she gotten to you?"

Chris sunk his head. "Of course,"

"And what did you do about it? What of the consequences?"

"I don't know. The Shadow never told me what would happen. It's easy to get bored."

"Then why bother being so protective about her with me," Vic said. "You make me feel like I'm missing something."

"You haven't made your choice. She's twisting you in her web so she can celebrate an upheaval. The balance of power in Oak Hollow will shift from the Curioso to the Creeper indefinitely."

"Why does she bother deluding you if you're a Curioso?" Vic asked.

"I could be deluding you, too. You never know."

Vic's closed his eyes. "What?"

"That's the point. You can't trust anyone. Our power's difficult to regulate or control. Especially knowing that our past baggage takes us to unspeakable depths."

"What are you trying to tell me?"

"I told you I got weak," Chris said. "I didn't have the discipline to keep resisting. Eventually, she and I had a bit of a falling out. When the Shadow told me I could take on a new mentee, I jumped at the occasion."

Vic smiled at Chris. "Correction... you 'hopped' at the occasion,"

"I see what you did there. Yes, I wanted to own you as my protégé, to teach you the way of the Curioso. Agatha doesn't deserve you. You're too brilliant to be owned by a half-life witch."

"Well, what does that make *you*?"

"That's for me to know," Chris said. "I've got to address something that has come up. Why don't you just stay here and rest a while?" He walked away.

CHAPTER THIRTY-FIVE

VIC RAMSEY was indeed weary, his mind racing from the lingering scenes observed in the hops. As Wilkerson moved about the corridor and out of sight, Vic wandered through the hallway, nearly knocking over a large barrel.

What are these things full of? Gosh, they're heavy. I hope they haven't checked anyone else in my room yet. I don't want to walk in on anyone.

Moving through the darkened hallway, he climbed back through the window of six-o-five. The room was reset to its default setup.

He cursed as the Riverton evening sky shined through the south window. "They took my stuff."

I'm in my room. I'm moving around of my own volition. In this existence, what do I have to lose? Can I break the glass? Can I slit my throat? Can I still pick up stations on the dust-bunnied Super Zenith? Where are my limits?

Running out into the hallway, he found his way to the opposite end and let out a yell. A man came through carrying a briefcase toward the area but moved straight past him, refusing to acknowledge him. The man entered the elevator. Trailing behind him, Vic also got on. He harassed the man, offended by his lack of response, standing close, and tapping him on the shoulder. There was simply no acknowledgment. As the elevator dinged and he proceeded into the lobby, Vic remained immobile — blocked and held back by something he could feel but never see. The doors closed up, and the elevator returned him to the sixth floor.

As the elevators opened, he studied an elongated corridor with rock walls and minimal lighting. A voice whispered something unintelligible. Moving toward it, his heart pounded, faster and faster.

What's going on? I thought I was... where are my nitros?

He walked through the dark corridor, searching for a pathway out.

Is that the Shadow?

Puffing smoke in the air, the figure moved toward him.

"Break through the barriers, Ramsey. Follow me," he called, taking a puff on a cigar as he went into the room.

I've got no willpower left, he thought. *I'm beat.*

Letting defenses down, Vic's seeming depletion of energy restored in a moment's time. He entered from the dark corridor into the center hallway, moving back toward six-o-five. The door remained a fine mahogany. He entered without knocking.

The Shadow sat at the desk in the corner where Vic had written his review. He peered into Vic's eyes, pouring a glass of *Old Tymer's*. "This floor," he said, "this place... it's a tricky thing, you see. I never could have imagined what my son would do with our beloved Oak Hollow. Once a plush field of lilies, sturdy oaks, and long forgotten streams replaced by a subway tunnel. Darned city developments undoubtedly leading to profits and gains. Sad truth is we lost touch with our origins."

Vic released his pent-up breath, remaining speechless while in the presence of the Shadow.

"I guess it's about time we had a chat," he said, nodding his head. "Yes. I'm talking to you, Vic Ramsey."

Vic pointed toward himself. "To me?"

"Take a seat. We might as well. Here, take a puff. Compliments of the house... rather, my son's house." The Shadow leaned toward Vic, handing it over. "I let Wilkerson take you to school on this dimension because I thought I could trust him, Vic."

"Yes... It's been... enriching. Can you tell me what's going on? I feel like I'm still missing something."

"I know you're not sure who to trust," the Shadow muttered. "Glimpses into fractured pasts you can't recall. People you feel like you've never met. It's bound to be overwhelming."

Vic puffed on the cigar as a wave of unspoken relief came over him.

"It's a peyote cigar. It'll cure what ails ya," the Shadow said. "So, tell me why you're here. Who you are...?"

"I'm here because I'm reborn as one of the six victims..."

The Shadow raised his eyebrows. "Is that what you think?"

"That's what I'm told."

"Vic, think this through with me," he said, moving closer. "Don't you recall your past? Your childhood. Your parents. The things that led you here?"

"I suppose I do."

"Do you still remember a defining moment that reshaped your entire life? Does it still replay in your mind's eye every single day?"

"Yes."

"Does that include a pagan search for finding yourself while in a dark tunnel?"

"I think so."

The Shadow pulled his chair closer to Vic, shaking his head. "It's got to be more concrete than that. Oak Hollow is tricking your mind like it does the rest. She owns and manipulates. The longer you linger, the more your most private thoughts are erased — and replaced with those of the people it's already stolen away."

"I want to believe you, sir, but I need proof."

"Faith... the substance of things hoped for... the evidence of what's not seen," the Shadow said. "Ever heard that before?"

"I suppose I have. I know it's not original..."

"No more supposing. Concrete answers. Walk with me. You have more freedom than you think. At the end of this hall is a door. Cross on through, and you'll see."

Vic's eyes narrowed. "Can you give me a reason to trust you?"

"You've seen enough. I've been around since it all began. Follow me."

They passed through the door, walking down flights of stairs.

"We've moved into a storage room in the tunnel. We won't linger. Creeper Joe piled the fifty-four in here before they decayed. So, I prefer not to loiter. Despite their soul's separation, there's still unspeakable struggle in this room. Do you remember coming down before?"

"It feels familiar," Vic said.

The door opened. The spring and waterfall area stood before them. The Shadow raked his hand across the top of it, splashing water from it onto his face.

"Come back to the beginning... I can see it in your eyes. You haven't *truly* tasted of the spring, and, Victor Jolon Ramsey, you are worthy of it. Agatha played you when you were here before — leaving you a victim of untimely circumstances."

Vic shook his head. "I don't understand."

"The old souls and caretakers of this land have a storied past, inevitably bringing us all back to their roots many times over. It's a penance those privy to such must pay."

"A penance?"

"Yes. An atonement," the Shadow said, picking up a pewter cup and dipping it in the spring. He handed it to Vic, and he drank from it. The waterfall just behind the pool reflected the past.

"Let it take you. It's the rule of the Spring of Life, the place we are now. You give to Oak Hollow. It gives back to those it deems worthy."

***

A pale-faced man stood in the middle of a sweat lodge, shaking hands with an old man of indigenous Chipequan origin. The men embraced, beginning an unfamiliar chant in unison. They inhaled bursts of smoke until the pale-faced man leaned in and squeezed the Chipequan elder tighter and tighter across the top of the flames burning beneath. Their spirits leapt from their bodies, intertwining in a cloud of smoke as they disappeared. To the right of the fire, an infant laid on the ground — its cry, shrill and distinct. A woman came into the sweat lodge, picking up the child, trying to assess his origin.

"Harold? Shaman? Where are you?" she asked.

Her tears dripped onto the face of the child. She pulled him close as his eyes became aglow. The salty discharge rolled off the infant's cheeks to the ground beneath, forming a hole in the earth, and creating a void that would become the spring.

Vic's eyes focused on the waterfall running behind the spring and its mysterious recirculating flow.

The Shadow remained to his right, staring toward him as he puffed on a cigar.

"Wednesday, October 29th, 1856. That's the day it all started," the Shadow said. "My relatives cheated their way into this land, and it's been cursed ever since."

"What are you trying to tell me?"

"What you saw is up to your interpretation. The Spring of Life is something special, formed by an incomparable bond. My son and I found it years ago, and though it took me with it that day, I knew it was right. I don't think it's been properly used, though."

"By you?" Vic asked.

"By anyone..."

CHAPTER THIRTY-SIX

NANCY HELBENS waited for her mother to arrive.

In all reality, revenge on mom seems a low cost in exchange for Randy, she thought. *Agatha's mind games are a minefield of unexpected destruction. They always were to mom.*

"Nancy, what are you trying to do?" Randy asked, looking up into her eyes.

She swatted Randy on the rear end. "I told you to stop calling me that."

"That's what you want me to believe. No good mom would whack her sweet boy," he said, imitating Agatha.

Nancy shook her head and grabbed Randy by the temples as she stared into his eyes. "That witch hexed your mind, boy. When this day's over, we're going to take you to a priest, and have him splash the holy water all over you and pray the evil away."

He spit toward her, cocking his fist back to sock her. "That's not going to happen, Nancy Helbens."

"Stop calling me that."

His eyes grew darker. "And if I don't? Are you going to punish me?"

I could slap you silly. Little defiant brat.

"You don't get to find out yet. That's for me to figure out," she said, her voice raising.

He pulled at the side of her blouse. "Did you *ever* claim me as your own, lady? Because, I don't remember that."

Nancy shoved him away. "Randy, stop it, now. Your behavior's going to land you on the medicine just like your father. Is that what you want?"

Bobbie Helbens appeared outside the entryway to the hotel.

"Look, Nancy. It's grandma," Randy said, his smile unfamiliar.

"That's enough!" she yelled. "Stay inside and watch the television." Moving toward the door, she motioned to Bobbie to come inside from behind the glass."

The old woman shook her head at Nancy. "I'm sorry, honey. I told you I'm not supposed to... going to come in."

What do you mean? There she goes with the 'honey' again. Ugh.

"I'll meet you out there," Nancy said. She pushed the buzzer to lock the door behind her.

Walking outside, she nodded her head toward her mother, motioning her to follow her.

"There's a break area at the back of the property, mom. We can share a smoke if you like."

"After our most recent chats, I could use a good smoke... What about Randy?" Bobbie asked. "I saw him in there watching the television."

"He'll be fine, mom. I engaged the security lock."

"Aren't there other guests checked in the hotel? There could be criminals... offenders. You're just going to let the tube babysit him?" Bobbie asked, her voice growing shaky.

"None any worse than you! Quit trying to be the parent you never were to me with my own. You don't get a second chance on that. I'm your report card. Your 'project' was turned in twenty some-odd years ago."

Nancy lit up the cigarette and took a puff. She handed the second one to her mother.

You are getting old, aren't you? she thought.

"Since when are we close enough to have a chat? Last time we talked, you kicked my ass to Timbuctoo."

"Since now," Nancy said, her flushed cheeks showing. "You showed up over here, didn't you? I guess you're desperate enough..."

"And why do you say that? You told me Randy needed someone to watch him. I'd never turn away a chance to watch that sweet boy."

Nancy crossed her arms as Bobbie puffed on the cigarette. "I made a deal with one of your old friends."

"Count my lucky stars," Bobbie grabbed Nancy by the arm, and leaned in closer — her voice dropping to a whisper, "Swear to me you didn't."

Nancy scoffed. "Who else would it be other than someone from your old women's club?"

"I left her in the dust, Nancy. You remember that, right? She kept begging for more and more of my time and my energy, and I couldn't give it to her anymore. It wasn't fair to you or to me to do it any differently."

Nancy furrowed her brow. "It's easy to paint with a broad brush looking back years later, and the funny thing is, we always paint ourselves prettier than anyone else. Don't we?"

"Nancy Helbens! That's about enough. I'm leaving now. You can never understand what I went through for you."

Where are you, witch? Let's get this finished, she thought.

"What's there to understand?" Nancy asked. "I know you had a rough childhood, and I'm sure that people couldn't have treated you well as homely as you've always been."

"Nancy, that's not appropriate."

"I'm sorry. 'Everyone has to vent now and then.' Isn't that what Agatha used to say to you. You picked out some real winners as friends, mom. I could keep going down the list," she said, cupping her hand over the side of her mouth and whispering, "because it's not that long."

"Are you stalling me? What's the delay? I'm going to get Randy and load him up."

"Good luck with that, mom. He's been acting strange lately."

CHAPTER THIRTY-SEVEN

VIC RAMSEY explored the tunnel behind the Shadow, moving toward the far end. They came upon the skeletons, jammed beneath the roots of an old oak tree that sprawled in every direction. Each one intertwined in its own unique way.

The Shadow paced back and forth, looking around.

"Is everything okay?" Vic asked.

Hesitating to reply, he faked a smile. "Everything's fine. I just wanted to show you where I relocated the skeletons."

"I brought them back here, along with the missing sixth," the Shadow said. "The place they belong — You know something, though? I always found it odd that the tree didn't die after the explosion."

"I thought the sixth skeleton was gone..."

"It doesn't work that way. You've hopped through Joe, have you not? The soul is gone, but the bones remain a reminder."

"Hmm. I was wondering how that worked if he was truly gone."

"Agatha's always claimed the sixth as her own, keeping it separate from the rest here in the tunnel. I've decided I can no longer allow that to continue. I let Chris keep the others on the sixth floor because it's a safe space to hop with minimal interruptions."

"Why not just keep Wilkerson down here?"

"Wilkerson is safe in the hotel. Not down here. I'm still coddling him a little. No one said I couldn't have a favorite..."

"And the sixth skeleton?"

"Yes. Agatha's bound to come looking for it soon. She performs regular rituals with the bones to validate herself, but it's all in vain."

"Aren't you concerned she'll come after us?" Vic asked.

The Shadow puffed on his cigar. "This is my dominion, Vic. You needn't concern yourself."

"Where do *I* fit into this?"

"I never said you did. That was just a bunch of smoke and mirrors from Chris. Far too often, we take matters in our own hands and fail to trust the hand that should guide us."

"What are you getting at?"

"This is the place the old bones belong," the Shadow said, straightening out the arm of one. "The place they were killed. One thing I've learned watching over this land — death lingers in the southeast corner. We shouldn't stay long."

Vic continued to study them closely.

"Something about the sixth one seems off."

"Maybe it is," the Shadow said. "And unless you know the differentiating physical features, you wouldn't know who was who, would you?"

Vic wrinkled his nose. "I suppose not."

The Shadow tipped his top hat to Vic. "What if I told you there were seven? That some of the change-ups were intentional..."

"I'm sorry. I don't understand."

"There were seven skeletons. Only six were restored, the sixth coming with a caveat."

Vic's eyes widened. "Which is? What is the caveat?"

"This is where our time must end."

"No," Vic said, fidgeting in his pockets. "I have to know."

"You don't understand, because you never belonged here in the first place. I've told you too much, already."

"What's the point of my being here, then?"

"None of us are above reproach, Vic. That 2-5 a.m. nonsense, you becoming a Curioso. All that was a sham to keep you under his thumb and study you. Chris lied to you."

"Lied to me?" Vic shook his head. "But why?"

"I didn't stop him. I was curious where it would lead, too. It's a lonely existence. He messed with your head a little, probably even slipped you a mickey. Convinced you that you were more than you were."

"Says the guy who gave me a peyote smoke?" Vic said, his face growing flushed. "I don't understand. I hopped... Saw flashes of the past... I heard people's thoughts. The scenes are still circling my brain like they were my own."

"I'm not disputing what you saw. That was all real. Hopping has nothing to do with your state of being, though. It's the beings themselves that carry the magic in their old bones. The property's legacy does the rest."

"Okay," Vic said. "I guess I'll buy that."

Chris Wilkerson emerged from behind a darkened alcove in the tunnel. "Vic," he said, "I tried to break it to you nicely earlier. Count your blessings you can still breathe. You brushed elbows with us — even got a flavor of what life could be like, and then just like that, we're going to let you get back to it."

"My life?" Vic said, rubbing his chin. "What did you have to gain? Why screw around with me this long if I'm as good as useless to you?"

"The sixth seat can never be filled again," the Shadow said, "but it makes for a good caper."

Vic scoffed. "I don't believe this... just like that, you break your own Cardinal Rule? Question... who enforces them if *you* can't even follow them? Is it a wicked scheme? Maybe. Have you lied? Absolutely. Permitted innocent blood to be shed? Guilty. Disrespected those that are lesser? Yep. Stirring up trouble in the community? That's for sure. Where do we even start? The enforcers are as guilty as the offenders."

"What are you trying to say? I didn't realize that you..." the Shadow said, his eyes narrowing. "You know I could stomp your throat out if I wanted to?"

"Yes, I know about the rules. Calhoun even wrote an article about it earlier in the year. He snapped a photo of the old cornerstone in the basement. No one flocked to it, though. You know why?"

"Why?" the Shadow asked, his face souring.

"I had it pulled. We never published it. I just had a bad feeling about it, and I told my editor the same thing. Calhoun was dead within a week. I stuffed it in one of my scrapbooks at home."

Chris swooped his hair back. "Hmm..."

"The souls deserve to rest," Vic said. "There's no point in prolonging their misery."

The Shadow's face remained blank.

Vic turned toward Wilkerson. "Chris, haven't you had your fill? I know you're bound to be worn from all you've shouldered and seen. I can see it. I can feel it."

"It's been a long while."

Walking toward the place where the dynamite had killed the victims, he leaned against one of the large roots of the oak above. "My mother was a Chipequa.

Somewhere deep within, I feel her spirit longing for closure, too, and she's been dead and gone for years."

"Is that a fact?" the Shadow asked.

Vic smiled. "In Chipequan culture, no one's ever buried. They're always burned. The bones can't stay. We have to carry them out of here to purify the land... There's no priest that can fix it. No magic words. Innocent blood's been spilled long after the rules were set. This needs to be done."

Chris kicked the ground repetitively. "No. No. No."

"That would make for a nice sappy ending. Wouldn't it?" the Shadow asked, as he subtly stepped back.

Vic moved closer toward them. "It's not too late to make up for the sins of the past. I'll help you. Bring what's been in the darkness into the light. You guys made something simple a heck of a lot more complex than it had to be. If you'd paid better attention, you would have realized that Chipequa are mystical, family-oriented people who relish upon the past. It only makes sense that the unexplained mysteries of this land would endure a prolonged struggle."

"What about the spring?" the Shadow asked. "My son and I found it."

Vic chuckled. "You still think *you* discovered it when you dug for a well? Didn't it strike you as odd that it came so easily to you? It was already there! It was just barely covered up. How naïve can you be? The spring revealed your origin to me as I drank from it."

"And what did you see?" the Shadow asked.

"You took on the role of the Shaman for this land many years ago. You never understood your purpose, though. Did you?"

"Shaman? I don't think so. How is that possible?"

"You didn't make yourself visible enough," Vic said. "How much good can a being with that much power do locked away in a basement? Or in this case, a tunnel. I'm reminded of an old poem.

"Go ahead, then."

"You hear many voices, but they never connect with you. You see many faces, but they never know you. You speak many meaningful words, but they never resonate within you."

"These are nice thoughts, Vic," the Shadow said, "but putting this into practice is not so simple."

"Why not? I saw your birth in the sweat lodge. A beautiful union of a Chipequan and a European immigrant materializing an incredible harmony in a second's time. Here we are, years later, a bastardized mess of what's left."

"Very good. Perhaps, we haven't given you your due credit," the Shadow said, scratching the top of his balding head.

Chris looked toward the Shadow. "I've looked up to you all this time when I should have pointed my faith somewhere else."

"Coulda. Shoulda. Woulda," the Shadow said. "Waste no more time fretting on it."

"Exactly," Vic agreed. "Let this be the path to righting the wrong."

"Fine. I'll let you take the bones," the Shadow said. "I've held onto them for selfish reasons."

"How can we do this right?" Vic asked.

"Now, suddenly, the man with 'all the answers' turns back to the wise old man?" the Shadow asked. "Why should I tell you? O enlightened one."

"Chipequan culture tells me so. You'll lose your place as Shaman and be replaced."

"Simply impossible."

"Believe what you want," Vic said, "if you ask me, the stage is set just the way Agatha wants it. She'll dominate it in her own way. Do you find it a coincidence that numbers are sacred here? Why were you gifted six followers? Why fifty-four deaths? Why fifty-four years to prove yourself before you died right here on the same property you were born? The questions are endless... and the sad truth is. You still don't have a definitive answer. Do you?"

"I don't."

"I'll help you. Again, it's Chipequan tradition. Our own ancient texts... *Be wary of increments of three, six, and nine. They are all but portals to self-destruction.*"

Agatha came down the tunnel, approaching the men as she cackled into the air. "Sorry, Will. While you were in the hotel, I took your skeleton away from the roots. I pitched your bones into the spring earlier and they disintegrated to little shards. I guess you're not worthy, anymore." She threw a piece at him. "From your cranium."

"Why would you do that?" he said, hanging his head.

"I knew you wouldn't be needing them anymore. You're all but dust and ash. Let the sun set, old man. Your time to shine's over."

The Shadow crumbled away.

"Chris, there's no point in holding back your secrets anymore, either," she said as he stood thunderstruck. "You were built to be a Creeper... All this balance of power talk is nonsense. The Creeper and the Curioso are nothing but a load of folklore — soon to be extinct outside this dominion. I've been listening. Let's carry these bones into the light and see what the earth has to say. It seems only fitting."

Chris backed away as his eyes began to glow. Agatha handed him a pewter cup.

"Drink up," she said, her smile a path to further agony.

CHAPTER THIRTY-EIGHT

Chris and Agatha collected the bones together, loading them into two large bags as they climbed up a ladder and toward the tunnel hatch. VIC RAMSEY sat below them, observing.

I'm not sure why they are ignoring me, he thought. *I guess I'll let them enjoy their moment.*

"Are you afraid of what's going to happen?" she asked.

"No. I've seen enough. If it's my time, it's my time. You?"

"A day of reckoning happens only once," she said, looking at Chris. "We'll see what mother nature has to say." They climbed out of the tunnel.

A separate skeleton sat in a darkened corner.

They left this one here. How did Wilkerson not see it? Well, here goes...

Vic walked over and grabbed hold of its right shoulder, hopping on his own.

***

Our link is inexplicable. I've merged the past with the present and it's overwhelming to me. Here I go again, watching him light the dynamite. The others, all innocent victims of his mania. Maybe a voice screamed from the great depths to distract him, or a depressed thought overwhelmed him from generations of poor care and he just finally snapped. It's hard to say. I revisit the moment again, knowing my link with him is special, perhaps even what pushed him over the edge. It's a little sickening. I laugh to myself for a moment and find myself in a dizzying haze. The origins of the old are merged with the traditions of new as the earth envelopes me whole.

Little Randy makes his way into the basement while his mother mans the front desk. I sneak in, finding my way to him. I hypnotize him to purge his memories of our fifty-four precious days together. He doesn't remember me at all, certainly not my face. I kept it covered, my eyes concealed as we presented him to the earth again like we tried at Bobbie's when the timing wasn't right. I only brainwashed her twice, and that's all it took for us to perform our ritual on the boy. I hadn't seen her in years. It was a little awkward, and in all reality, it probably should have felt that way. I set the metronome that night and erased it away so she wouldn't feel the burden of my visits. It was a one and done event. Okay, fine, two and done. Randy deserved it. I waited for mother earth to call for him and follow her order, covering him with layers and layers of topsoil. The thought of harming him overwhelms me. My instincts struggle, never knowing where my limits are. Is Randy the sacrifice the earth demands? She already paid her respects once to him that night in her basement [just like the days of old] — the soil soaking into his skin and cleansing him from his own thorn — a generational habit of anger so suppressed it could only explode at the worst of times. The sad truth is, the boy hides it so well. *How could she struggle to know the child?* I've seen this before. Ask Bobbie Helbens. The two couldn't have been further from one another. From the moment Nancy was born, she was predestined to a tough life, and all the while made Bobbie's tougher. I watched her tireless efforts to purify Nancy with elements of the earth, making the child despise her more, doing everything in her power to avoid the ritual. I remember one of our basement gatherings years ago. Thank heavens Mitch was gone. Our little earth loving society smocked up and went toward Nancy — laying hands, chanting the fifty-four incantations of the ancient earth. It was all just a faithful pursuit to better living. Something the people of Riverton had long shunned.

I call out to Randy. "Hey, son. Mother's been looking for you."

"She is?" he asks, his innocent eyes far too trusting.

"Yes," I say. "Follow me into the tunnel. I'll show you."

It's easier than I can fathom. Perhaps my charming face is more trustworthy than I thought. Or, maybe the poor kid is just tired of the ping pong relationship of Nancy and what's his name. I continue to manipulate the boy. One lie at a time. It's not really a lie. It's misdirection. It's essential I stress that. I'll eventually lead the boy to the truth. He deserves to hear it.

"Come on in. Mommy will make you a grilled cheese and some tomato soup over the fire," I say, smiling at him as his grin cracks.

It's troublesome how easy it is. My mind wanders to all the criminals, crooks, and kidnappers and their troublesome ways. I sympathize with the beautiful children. Far too neglected by their families to know the difference between good and evil. And that... is the difference between my kind of evil and theirs. A good mother will protect her own. So many of them fail to live out their purpose. It's a downward spiral down a troubled slope — a path to endless disappointment.

"Here's your grilled cheese, Randy," I say, hugging him close to me. "It's nice to have a mommy who cares more about you than going to work. Isn't it?"

"Thank you," he says, his smile telling a story I never want to stop. The void in my heart has been filled.

"Let me teach you to paint, son," I say. "Follow me over here."

"Okay," he says, studying the canvases I have out for him. I see him struggling.

"They look different from the kind I'm used to seeing," he says.

I smile at him. "They *are* different, Randy. The skin from our bodies makes the finest canvases. When someone dies, I give them an opportunity to be cherished and loved forever. I dry out the skin — scoring, firing, and drenching it in a variety of fluids. Then I mount it over wood framing to give the appearance of one you'd buy at the store. It's heavier than the kind Nancy might have used when you were younger, but that's okay. Mommy will teach you to use this one. We'll start with the red."

His eyes are terrified as he struggles to find words.

I sing to him, "Red and yellow, black and white... they are precious in His sight..." He looks at me, his smile softening.

"What? You never heard that song before?" I ask.

He shakes his head. "No."

"What a shame," I reply. "A good mommy would have taught you that one. We're all precious in the sight of our maker. Every last one of us."

"We are?" he asks, his sweet face showing genuine intrigue.

"That's why I'm teaching you now."

"So you can be a better mommy?" he asks.

I smile at him and rub his shoulder. "That's exactly right, my boy."

CHAPTER THIRTY-NINE

NANCY HELBENS watched Bobbie as she waved at Randy at the hotel entrance and whispered in his ear.

What are you saying to my boy? Good kid... don't go with her.

Bobbie approached her Taurus, avoiding further eye contact with Nancy.

As she started the engine and put her seatbelt on, Agatha emerged from behind the storage building. She waved at Nancy, moving toward Bobbie. Her glowing eyes made Nancy's heart skip a beat.

Finally!

Walking toward the vehicle, she walked with a graceful and effeminate elegance. She tapped on the window of the vehicle with the tips of her sharp fingernails. Bobbie rolled it down slowly. "I didn't expect to see *you* again anytime soon."

Agatha grinned. "Is that a fact?"

"What's in the black bag you got there?" Bobbie asked, her brow furrowing.

"Pieces of the past, honey."

She pulled out the bone and tapped Bobbie on the shoulder with it.

"It's about time we leave *you* in the dust, like you did me," Agatha sneered. "Your time's up, Bobbie Helbens."

The authority in Agatha's voice made Bobbie crumble away into the car seat as the sunlight shined upon the bone.

"Oh my gosh," Nancy said, her face losing color as she studied the ash in the seat.

She peered toward Agatha, perplexed by her mother's peculiar demise. As tears trickled down her cheeks, she walked toward the woman as she closed the Taurus door, and the witch spread her arms wide.

"Come to mommy, sweetheart. Hug it out with me," Agatha said, wrapping her arms around Nancy tightly.

I feel so relieved and indebted, she thought. *Thank you.*

As Nancy's mind relaxed, she lost touch with reality, overcome by emotion in the moment with Agatha, and finding rest in her arms.

She reassured Nancy with her caressing hand. "It's okay, now. Things are going to be better."

Chris Wilkerson stumbled out of the tunnel hatch.

Wilkerson? I haven't seen you in years...

He carried what looked to be a heavy black bag.

"Chris? Is that you?" she asked, her jaw dropping as she wiped her tears away.

Peering toward her a moment, his eyes glowed, flashing a grin she hadn't seen before. "I should have never lied about you," she said to Chris.

Relief in your eyes. That's what you needed to hear.

Wilkerson dumped the bones into the dirt. He crumbled away as the sunlight hit them.

"It was his time to move on from this life, darling," Agatha said. "I can see you need some nurturing. Come with mommy."

Mommy?

Agatha leaned over the black bag of bones, picking one up and holding it in the light.

"I'm still here. Ha-ha! I'm one with the earth."

"Let me see that," Nancy said, studying the bone closer. "It has an O on it."

Agatha pursed her lips. "It... what?"

"There's an O marking on the bone. What's it to you, anyway?"

"Forget it..." Agatha said. "When are you going to own the truth?"

"What truth?"

"We both know Randy's not yours. He never was. I know it's sad, Nancy, facing the fact that you were never fertile... and neither was Bobbie. But *I* was... both times."

"Agatha... I don't see how this can be..."

"It just is, Nancy. You and I both know that you two never bonded the way you should have, but you and me, we can have forever."

Nancy shook her head. "No... this can't be. Mom had all these photos of me nursing with her and so on."

"You called her a sociopath yourself. It was all a show, honey. You know it was. It's bound to be making more sense now. Why else would I prey on your kind? Accept the truth. A lying tongue will never get us anywhere, will it? Nowhere but in trouble. The truth speaks for itself. Come back into the tunnel and drink from the spring again, child. I know you had a few swigs before. The tunnel was once your home too, right?" Agatha said, smiling. "Now that the Shadow's crossed over and it's in my care, we can be young together forever. A mother and daughter with a bond more special than any could ever know!"

CHAPTER FORTY

VIC RAMSEY went down a list on his notepad. Speculation was the best he could do.

My list...

First skeleton, Steve Renzell, alive, suspected Curioso. (O)
Second skeleton, Bobbie Helbens, alive, suspected Creeper. (X)
Third skeleton, Chris Wilkerson, reborn, suspected Curioso. (O)
Fourth skeleton, Mary Cathel, reborn, unknown. (X)
Fifth skeleton, Creeper Joe, reborn, now crossed over, former Creeper. (X)
Sixth skeleton, Agatha Haney, reborn *(unknown caveat), suspected Creeper. (X)

She's left her own skeleton in here, but why? She's more than willing to bring the rest in the light. Seven skeletons. Seven skeletons. If she's reborn, what makes her any different from the rest?

His mind wandered as he picked up the intact skeleton.

I remember the youth I saw in her face as she came up from the spring before. The bones. The sixth skeleton's never been brought into the light. They don't go together. Why don't I give you a taste of your own medicine? It worked on the Shadow.

He dropped the bonded bones into the spring and the skull snapped away from the spine.

The unnatural merge of the two left the bones bubbling to a boil and separating into tiny fragments with exception to the skull. It launched upward through the top of the tunnel.

The area brightened as sun shined through the growing hole that formed above, illuminating the Spring of Life for the first time in ages.

That's better. I need to get out of here.

***

NANCY HELBENS followed Agatha down into the tunnel through the hatch, struggling to cope with the difficult truth presented her. A pile of shattered bone fragments floated in the Spring of Life as its water slowly dried up.

"Look at the light shining through," Nancy said.

Agatha shrieked. "This can't be. My bones are drying up the spring, drinking up all that's left. Get a few swigs with me, honey, before it's too late."

Agatha grabbed her pewter cup, sipping from the spring as quickly as she could as her youth momentarily rejuvenated.

"Look at how beautiful I am when it's fresh, sweetheart. This can be *your* youth again, too, Nancy!"

Nancy shook her head. "It's all yours. You need it more than I do."

Agatha smiled at Nancy. "How sweet of you." As she sipped on the spring's final droplets, she chanted a Latin incantation. "This will keep it vital," she said, looking toward Nancy as she took another sip. Her skin sagged, her drooping wrinkles removing her superficial youth and figure, and returning it to her naturally born eighty-year-old self. Her power was reduced to an unending mortality as an old woman. Her date of birth, October 29th, 1910, – the date of William Wasserman's untimely death in Oak Hollow.

Nancy looked at Agatha. "Well, *mom*... old age can be a real bitch, can't she?" she said, laughing as she looked toward the dried-out waterfall and spring as Agatha's face continued to age.

CHAPTER FORTY-ONE

VIC RAMSEY found his way back through the passage in Greenwich's office. The Cardinal Rules remained posted to the wall. He kicked the cornerstone, and it crumbled as black oil trickled through into the basement.

We're going to pretend that didn't happen. The hair on the back of his neck stood straight up. Walking swiftly through the basement, he went upstairs.

He went past a red-headed boy that stood in the lobby.

"Hey, mister," the boy said. "What were you doing in the basement?"

"Just exploring. I'm a guest of the hotel. What's it to you, little man?"

"I saw you in the tunnel before. I'm just a curious kid. It's nothing to me."

"Fair enough," Vic said, stopping by the front desk. "I'm on my way out of here. I'll just grab some of this stationery, a couple of these black inked Bics, and I'll be on my way."

The boy nodded. "That works. I think my mommy's outside. I'll go out there with you."

Vic patted the boy on the head. "Who am I to stop you? It's a free country. Liberate the children!"

Randy stared toward Vic. "I like your sense of humor. My name's Randy."

Vic extended his hand. "Vic Ramsey. A pleasure to meet you, Randy. Give my regards to your mother when you get a chance."

Randy's eyes glossed over, appearing perplexed by the innocent comment.

"I sure will, mister. Take care!"

They waved goodbye to one another.

As Vic walked outside, he saw another man pulling up in a puke green Daihatsu.

What a crapmobile.

"Daddy!" Randy yelled. Ron Richards ran toward him.

"I wasn't sure where you or your mom were. When she didn't drop you off last night, I knew I had to come and check on you. I couldn't get a hold of her. I don't want either of you hanging around this place anymore, son. It gives me the creeps."

"Oh... daddy... I'm sorry. It's not scary anymore. Mommy took care of it."

Ron smiled at Randy. "I'm glad to hear that."

Randy looked toward the ground. "Dad, why are you wearing clown shoes?"

"The shoes are for my new job. I'm working down there at the nervous hospital."

"You're silly."

"I know... your old dad's got an impressive resume. Doesn't he? I don't think I'll ever settle on one job for too long. My radio gig at WGBO was lightning in a bottle. Maybe I'll get another shot. Anyhow, I'm going to see if your mom and I can patch it up. I got us conditionally approved for a mortgage on that house across town. The big fancy one we talked about..."

Ron looked toward Vic. "Randy, you want to introduce me to your friend?"

Gah. Why am I still loitering here? Vic thought. *Great, he thinks I'm some kind of kid loving weirdo.*

"Sorry, was just leaving. Vic Ramsey, Riverton Statesman. I was just finishing an article on the hotel."

"I'll be sure to watch for it," Ron said, his eyes rolling.

"You don't trust the newspaper media?"

"Why should I? You're all working an angle, aren't you? All of you guys are bought out by some big tycoon who wants to shove propaganda down our throats... I may sound crazy now, but I know the truth will find its way out one of these days. Just you wait..."

Let's not and say we did, Vic thought. *I'm starving.*

"Take care, then." Vic waved at them both, walking away toward the Bridgewater Restaurant up the block as the evening sky approached. He went inside. After the host motioned him to take a seat at the bar, he dropped his head a moment and studied the bartop. Its glossy finish had a variety of rings and discolorations from mugs, bottles, and glasses through the years.

The cantankerous bartender approached. "What's it going to be?" he asked, leaning in closer to Vic.

"I'll take the Ramsey Special."

"And what in the hell makes you think I'm going to remember what that is?"

"It's three ounces of cola and two ounces of *Old Tymer's*, stirred, never shaken," Vic said.

The bartender sighed. "I'll see what I can do."

A Flitz beer bottle slid across the bartop from the opposite end. Despite the impressive fifteen foot feat, the bottle neither spilled nor shattered to the floor.

Livewire approached Vic. "I was wonderin' if you'd ever come back."

"Me, too," Vic said, looking away.

"Is it that difficult lookin' another man in the eye?"

"I'm sorry. It shouldn't be."

The bartender clacked Vic's drink onto the bar. "There you go... a Damsel Special."

"It's... Ramsey Special," Vic muttered.

"That's what I said, a Damsel Special. Now drink up or get out."

Livewire grinned at Vic as he swigged his Flitz. "He ain't worth the time. You looked like you wanted to say somethin'."

"I do."

"From one Chipequa to another, I heard ya."

"I never connected enough with my mother before she was gone," Vic said. "I wish I would have."

"There's a piece of us that lingers after we're gone." Livewire pointed toward Vic's heart. "The Chipequa in our blood is buried deep — just waiting for the right voice to beckon."

The hum and chatter of Bridgewater grew louder as he finished his Ramsey Special.

"How was your stay, anyhow? Last I saw ya, you were about to check in."

"You were right. I checked in... I never had a proper check out, though."

Livewire gulped. "I'm sorry... What was that?"

"I had a less than conventional stay."

"Say no more. Your eyes tell a greater story. Bartender, get this man a Flitz."

"Sure thing, wiseguy," the bartender chirped.

What do I have to lose? He's a Chipequan.

"I want to talk to you about an idea I have," Vic said, sighing. "The forgotten shadows of the past must never again transcend the present in secret. I've been sitting on a nest egg for a long while, and I suppose I can afford to share some of it. I'd like to set up an anonymous donation in honor of the Chipequa natives that remain in this region. The property that The Oak Hollow Hotel rests upon must be returned to restore peace to the land."

Livewire clasped his hands. "The spirits linger. I don't think the Greenwich family could ever swallow their pride to hand it over. They were linked with the Wasserman's."

"Jerry's dead. William lost touch with his purpose. There's a new sh..."

"Stop right there," Livewire said. "Don't say another word."

"I don't understand," Vic said. "This is what I need to talk to you about. We found the skeletons... the remnants of your grandfather. I think it's time we give them a proper death ritual."

Livewire teared up. "The... the tunnel? Are you serious? How do you know?"

Vic stared toward the bartop as he spoke. "The souls lingered on in the lives of six others, rebirthed or given a second chance in a new body. I've seen into the past. We're talking decades of poverty and oppression, completely unfair to our heritage. It's natural to have complicated feelings. That kind of stuff passes on from one generation to the next. Maybe a touch of your grandfather's bones in the light of the sun will give you the closure you need."

"Take me to the bones, and I'll tell you for certain."

"No can do," Vic said. "I'm not going anywhere near that hotel again. Look around back. I'm sure you can find them. They should be somewhere in a black bag."

"It's best I get goin', then."

"I'll walk outside with you. I'm not going any closer to that hotel, though."

Vic dropped a five-dollar bill on the counter, and exited the building.

"That's better," the bartender mumbled.

An orange glow filled the sky as they came out of the restaurant.

The large oak tree standing behind the hotel blazed as its flames caught hold of the ground, racing toward it. Black oil ran down the sides of the structure, emerging from the sixth-floor windows as it caught fire.

"Do you want to call the fire department?" Vic asked.

"Do you?"

"Na..." Vic said, as they grinned toward one another. "Someone else will eventually. Let's hope everyone got out."

"It's funny..." Livewire mumbled, looking away from the scorch a moment. His eyes were wider and brighter. His voice, deeper and more articulate.

"What's funny?"

"We always knew the Wasserman's kept vats of oil stored away in there. Some of it even harvested from this very property before the subway. Only fitting, the place going up in beautiful flames like this."

"Is that right?" Vic asked.

Livewire's eyes remained glossed over a moment, before returning to their typical color and sheen. The timbre in his voice and speech pattern standardized.

"What was I saying? This fire did a number on me," Livewire said, clearly perplexed.

What just happened? Vic thought.

"You said the Wasserman's had oil in there."

"Huh? How would I know that? I wasn't alive back then," he said, walking away from Vic. He turned around. "Everybody gets their comeuppance, eventually. Right?"

Vic watched the blaze a second longer before walking back into Bridgewater. The block remained quiet.

After a night like this... another round won't hurt.

He found his way into the bar. "How about another Damsel Special?"

The bartender smiled. "You know something? You're not so bad, after all. One Ramsey Special coming right up."

FALL 1992

CHAPTER FORTY-TWO

LIVEWIRE stood nervously in the crowd, overwhelmed by the thought of speaking in public.

I don't want to do this. Why couldn't they pick someone else? he thought.

The Mayor of Riverton stood at 5454 Oak Hollow Lane. His voice came through the speakers loudly. "It's a special day today as we welcome a new generation of excitement on this once lovely property to celebrate the rich heritage of our past. Even flames won't squash that potential. I'm proud that we can join together and celebrate a proper revitalization to the Oak Hollow District and Old Town Riverton as it deserves. We have a special guest of Chipequan origin with us that we are going to honor. Bob James, please come to the podium."

Livewire walked up slowly, speaking into the microphone shortly after studying the crowd. "Thank you. It never fails, no matter how many times I try to tell people to call me Livewire; you all still call me 'Bob.' My mother took a Euro-American last name to move forward from our past, but let me tell you something, I still bleed Chipequan. The tribe is less known than we were in 1856 when we dispersed, breaking away into separate pieces, but our hearts remain united. I'd be lying if I didn't admit my grandfather's effect on my life. I never met the man, but the legacy and devastation from his actions continues to affect many of us years later, whether we want it to or not. It was overshadowed by fifty-four murders in the 1928 massacre at The Oak Hollow Hotel. But there was another 1928 massacre that happened here; as a matter of fact, it was later on the very same day. Grandfather's dissatisfaction with life and the mistreatment of the Chipequan's by the Wasserman family left him feeling disillusioned and disjointed from his ancestors. He was on the subway project when it began and long before it was forgotten. As they worked their way through the tunnel, blowing their way through more difficult sections, his ongoing struggles with depression led him to an uninteresting end, taking six others alongside him. The bodies were never recovered. I'm pleased to announce today, that the remnants of those recovered, along with my grandfather's can all be given the proper exit ritual they always deserved... They say it takes a village to resolve complex problems. I can't think of a better way to bring these problems to a close. As we conduct the ribbon cutting for the Chipequa Native Heritage Center, let me say on behalf of the entire Chipequa nation that we appreciate our benefactors, Riverton, and the Precinct Three Council commemorating our history and finally bringing honor to us. Let's take a moment to reflect on our ancestors and the sacrifices that gave us a chance to be here today." As he backed away from the podium, the crowd of onlookers shared a moment of solidarity while he peered upon the beautiful museum.

Approaching the microphone again, tears rolled down his cheeks. "Thank you for making me whole again. Years ago, a piece of me died in the tunnel beneath us when my grandfather died, and it never left me alone. I can now in great confidence say he's finally at peace, and I am, too. Let's enjoy this day and celebrate Chipequan heritage in Oak Hollow until the end of the age."

He turned around to cut the ribbon. The crowd applauded. He saw his grandfather beckoning him through the door of the museum.

Granddad?

The glass walls throughout the ground floor left the room wide open and bright as brilliant exhibits honored the region's Chipequan natives, finally casting them in a favorable light.

He looked around, admiring it a second before he saw his grandfather motioning him around a corner into his new office. The gold-plated placard was embossed in blue letters.

BOB "LIVEWIRE" JAMES
CHIPEQUAN CURATOR IN RESIDENCE

His eyes remained wide.

I don't believe this. How are you here?

"You can speak to me aloud, I won't be long," his grandfather said as he closed the door to his new office.

"Take a seat. Can you help me bring harmony to this cursed land once and for all? I assume that's why you're here?"

"As much as I'm proud to see what you're doing to preserve our culture and traditions, Livewire, I'm afraid I'll only let you down again. The walls surrounding us remind me of man's finite mortality and the overarching barriers of modern culture seeping in, choking the remaining life of our fathers away, day by day."

"Granddad, why are you so cynical?" Livewire asked. "Father always held you in such high esteem, bringin' honor to you all throughout my early years. Grandmother loved you dearly."

He covered his eyes, his hand resting on his forehead. "She brought us together, my son — admiring our contrast."

Livewire's face remained tense. "Huh? What you gettin' at?"

His grandfather nodded, biting his lower lip as he hesitated to speak. "I was young and naïve, a renegade of my family. In desperation to chase life with a beautiful foreigner, I abandoned the way of the Chipequa for the woman you knew as your grandmother, Henrietta."

"Don't be so hard on yourself. You loved her, right?"

"Well, of course I did, but I betrayed that," he said, picking up the brochure for the facility that showcased various cultural relics gathered. "I betrayed you all. Despite our beliefs and ideologies steeped in sororal polygyny, Henrietta's origins begged me to uphold my marriage to her in a sacred covenant with the imported tradition of monogamy."

"That's a mouthful, but I get it," Livewire said, nodding to his grandfather, "but father always told me that blowing up the men in the tunnel was a necessary casualty for you to offset their wrongs. You did what you thought was right, knowing the Chipequan bond with this land would forever be broken as the Wasserman's came in and modernized it. Right?"

His grandfather's eyes reflected a long wandering spirit. "You make it sound so much more political than it was, Livewire. Not everything has a double meaning... What's this world coming to? My spirit was willing, but my flesh was weak... and I gave in."

"Gave in to what? Your anger? Your fear? Why did they all have to die in the tunnel that night?"

"I laid with her one night — the night before I passed on."

A tear went down Livewire's cheek. "What's uncommon about that? It's primal."

"That's just it. They lied to you. Henrietta's younger sister, Agatha, studied the Chipequan traditions with jealousy as our marriage materialized. After many months and no pregnancy, my pride left me concerned of what message this would carry. What would it speak of my manhood to other men and their families? I would never embarrass Henrietta that way in public."

"What do you mean they lied to me? What are you tryin' to say?"

"The night before I ended it all, I drank from the spring in the tunnel we were digging, and it showed me incredible things of the future, even your future, of this very conversation in this special building. And in that moment of heightened pleasure, I violated the vow I made to my barren bride, thinking it to be the only way to carry on our family heritage."

"Oh, granddad," Livewire said, moving toward him and wrapping his arms around him.

His grandfather teared up. "I could never face the guilt – the reality of looking back into Henrietta's eyes when she found out how I betrayed her. Gazing into my eyes that night, Agatha offered herself to me to carry on the family name and I relented, justifying my actions by our common families. Bring the truth in the open once and for all. My soul's been trapped with Agatha for many moons. Wasserman tore us apart and then merged us together."

"What are you sayin'? You're startin' to sound crazy."

"The Shadow attached my skull to her spine. She never had complete control. I've been there with her, whispering in her ear, our souls aimlessly linked for all these years. A penance for our suicides. We were both unworthy. We could never have complete autonomy until our silver cord and golden bowl were severed, once and for all. I tried to show you. So many times, ever since that nice evening *we* had in '78 by the campfire."

Livewire's face grew flushed.

"I'm torn away from her agony, now. And, hopefully, she's torn away from mine. The spirits are calling me home, my son," he said, crumbling away to dust and ash.

***

While Livewire remained lost in thought, there was a tap on the door.

"Come in," he said.

Steve Renzell entered the room, his nametag reflecting under the light, S. RENZELL, MUSEUM DIRECTOR.

"What brings you in, sir?"

"I wanted to see how you were settling in. I just walked around and spoke words of blessing on the facility," Renzell said. "We have a lobby full of guests with a lot of questions and no one to answer them well. I've been fielding them as best as I can. Between us, I've been in the pawn shop business too long and I'm rusty at this sort of thing, but I'm honored at the privilege. It's going to take a while for me to change gears. Miss Cathel's working the ticket counter. I'd say she's due a break before long. Do you mind covering for her a while? Ramsey had to leave, but he said he would commit to doing five hours per week as a volunteer."

"Did he really? I'll give it my best." He walked into the museum gallery a changed man.

CHAPTER FORTY-THREE

VIC RAMSEY sat at his desk, drafting his next column. His small desk cassette deck played the latest *RUSH* album quietly. He was relieved to enter a new phase in his life, enlightened by his experiences in Oak Hollow, never returning but instead giving a substantial donation to form Riverton's newest museum and cultural experience.

After an interesting year and series of write-ups on The Oak Hollow Hotel, I see it fitting that we cherish the legacy of the Chipequa and celebrate the diversity of our city's leadership and private sources in spurring on a grant to fund and open the Chipequa Native Heritage Center. What a beautiful ceremony. The land was in the wrong hands for many moons. Do you believe in the significance of numbers? Nine is a special one... a number of universal love, karma, faith, and enlightenment. That's enough about that, though. All great articles start with potential until they go off the rails into a long-winded rambling where a journalist starts riffing on a soapbox. What I was getting to before, there's power in uncovering the mysteries of the past to make sense of the present. Sometimes it's painful, other times it's enjoyable, and it's therapeutic. They say pouring salt in a wound can hurt, but more often than not, we find ourselves ignoring it, just hoping it will heal on its own. My mother taught me a long time ago that the best way to heal is to know the pain, and to appreciate our normalcy when we aren't suffering. I don't mean to sound like a broken record. Not every momma's advice is wise, proud, or even applicable, but I'm thankful for the memories I have with mine. How about you?

P.S.: To my fallen colleague, you could have never known what The Oak Hollow Hotel had in front of you. RIP: Jake Calhoun, 1953-1991.

-VR

Lifting his hands from the typewriter, he studied the flickering light fixture above. A door across the room squeaked open and Hal Dorse called him into his office. As Vic approached, Hal tucked a Lucky Strike behind his right ear as he pushed one of Ramsey's doodles across the desk. Dorse's poker face was unreadable.

"It's time we have a chat," Dorse said. "Your future with the *Statesman* hangs in the balance."

Murphy's Law bites me in the ass, he thought. *What was that about karma?*

"The cleaning lady found this last year while you were at that hotel, and I kept it in my drawer. It reminded me we're all human—even me. I'd like to see you inspire the rest of the staff to avoid a demotion across town to the Anvil. What do you say? Will you do me the honor?"

"I'm sorry, what?"

Dorse grinned. "Ramsey, I'm hanging it up," he said, coughing in an uncontrolled fit. "The lung cancer's got me, and I want to spend my final days with my family. I'm going to recommend you for the senior editor post if you feel you're up for it. That remarkable number you did on The Oak Hollow Hotel put our newspaper back on the map. How's that for a fifty-fourth birthday present?"

What are you talking about?

"Thank you, sir. I don't know what to say. I can't say I quite pictured it ending this way."

"That you become an editor, or that I get lung cancer?" Dorse said, coughing exaggeratedly.

Vic laughed. "Well, a bit of both. I never followed the traditions of this institution or held any special loyalty to it. Why bother taking a risk on *me*?"

"We all have our moments. The best heroes are often the most unlikely."

Vic nodded his head. "I suppose I'd be a fool to answer any differently. I can't make any promises that I won't do some major overhauling on the paper format and its approach to presenting objective truth. It's certainly well overdue. If it's all the same to you, sir, I just wanted to clarify that before we moved forward with this discussion."

Dorse smiled, his face peaked as he replied, "That's not a problem, Ramsey. I need someone with a fresh perspective in the chair. You deserve a corner office. I'll send out a bulletin this afternoon, and my desk will be cleared out tomorrow."

"That sounds good."

"Hey," Dorse said, motioning to the door, "I've hired you a new receptionist. She's unconventional, a little on the seasoned side, but I'm told she's fantastic. Her long fingernails can type a hundred words per minute. Would you care to meet her?"

Vic nodded. "I suppose I would."

Concrete answers, Vic, he thought, smiling. *Don't you ever learn?*

They exited the office, moving into the reception. A woman's back was turned as she rifled through her purse. Her perfume smelled like gardenias, her hair snow white. The pin-striped pantsuit and starched oxford shirt she donned contrasted with the other receptionists in the office.

"Hi there..." Dorse said. "I want you to meet your new editor-in-chief and supervisor, Vic Ramsey. Vic, this is..." Making eye contact with the woman, Vic's heart pounded through his chest uncontrollably, and Dorse's voice faded away.

I left the nitros in the car... It's a beautiful time to unwind... it's a beautiful time to unwind... it's a beautiful time to...

He gagged. Collapsing to the floor, his spirit floated away while Dorse tried to perform CPR. While he approached the heavens, Dorse's annoying voice continued jabbering away.

"Agatha, I'm sorry. I guess he just wasn't cut out for the job."

She whispered under her breath while she adjusted her red framed glasses and tucked the chain back beneath her hair.

"I'm sorry... what?" Dorse asked.

"Victor never was a... momma's boy," she said. Her filed teeth twinkled as the reflection of the fluorescents hit them.

CHAPTER FORTY-FOUR

The lights on the former Reinhold estate were on again as NANCY HELBENS RICHARDS and Ron finished moving in with Randy. The home's extravagance remained too much for them, but it was an overdue escape from their cramped apartment.

"It's hard to fathom this deal coming through the way it did," Nancy said, carrying a box through the entryway. "I'm so glad we patched our marriage up, though. I love you, weirdo."

Smiling at Nancy, Ron leaned in and kissed her. "I didn't know dad had that much saved up to be honest. I guess it pays to be an only child," he said, taking off his WCBL 720AM ball cap. "It sure took a while for the courts to settle the distribution, though."

Randy ran up and down the halls of the new home in excitement.

Johnny Lathrop pulled into the front of the estate in his beat-up blue Cutlass Ciera. "Islands in the Stream" by *Dolly Parton* and *Kenny Rogers* blared through the worn car speaker as he came down the long driveway.

"Nancy, it's our song. Let's stop for a minute," Ron said.

Before she could come toward him, Johnny killed the engine, and the music cut off abruptly. He jumped out of the car, his hair freshly bleached, the large belt buckle atop his Levi's shimmering as the sun began to set.

"Congratulations, folks!"

Ron walked over to Johnny, shaking hands with him. "I figured you would have already blown your commission on a new ride. Why are you still in this hunk of junk?"

"It's still driving, Ramblin' Ron... That's what matters. Hey, I just want to say I heard your episode yesterday, talking about your glory days with Wayne Wallace, and I just have to ask... Will you guys ever team up again?"

"That's for us to decide," Ron said.

"Fair enough," Johnny replied, his Cheshire cat grin, wide. "I brought you a housewarming gift. I hope you like it."

He opened the back door to the vehicle as piles of empty fast-food cups and trash dropped to the ground.

"I'm sorry. I know I need to take it to the wash."

Get on with it, Nancy thought.

"You know I helped broker a deal on the hotel right before that crazy inferno? The Greenwich family was bankrupt. The closer gave me this old leather-bound book when we wrapped it up, asking me if I wanted it as a memento. I didn't know what to do with it? The Chipequa Museum people didn't want it. I think it's an old hotel policy manual. I figured since Nancy worked over there, she might appreciate having it. You know, to remember the olden days. I don't read much, so I haven't cracked it open. It's not what I would exactly call... light reading."

"What's your definition of light reading?" Nancy asked. "The Riverton swimsuit catalog?"

"Shut up!"

"Thanks." Ron laughed, taking the book. "Man, this thing is heavy."

Nancy waved and went inside, avoiding further verbal acknowledgment.

***

Falling into bed after a long day, Nancy studied the fan blades as they rotated. Randy was tucked in for the night and they finally had a moment to catch up. Ron was already lounging in his wife beater and boxer shorts with the television playing a *Night Watch* rerun as he leafed through The Oak Hollow Hotel policy manual.

"Why did you bring that old dusty thing in here, Ron? I don't want that. Living in an old house already cranks up the spook factor enough. Old relics can't help matters any."

"I'm still more concerned about a government sniper taking us out than I am a ghost," he said. "What's this mean? I don't see what it has to do with hotels."

He handed the book over, pointing to the page.

ALWAYS BE WARY OF UNEXPECTED SURPRISES. THERE'S ALWAYS A CATCH.

"I don't know and I don't care," she said. "I'm not going to let fear control my life anymore. That's all in the past."

She pulled the comforter closer toward her neck as coolness creeped into the room through the open window.

"Changing subjects a bit, Ron, I... I want to talk to you about something."

"About what?" he asked.

"Agatha... when you were *with* her, I mean 'with her, with her'... was it work? Or did you enjoy it?"

Ron sighed. "Nancy, you know I wanted to fulfill your wishes to have a family. As primal a man as I may have seemed, I could never go through with it. She gave me the creeps. Agatha found someone else to father Randy."

The color in Nancy's face escaped her. "Ron... please tell me you're lying."

"I'm sorry I never told you. But I didn't want it to change what we had. I thought our relationship was special, and I didn't want to see it fall apart because I didn't deliver," Ron said.

"That's just it, Ron," she said, sighing, as a tear rolled down her cheek. "I don't think it would have. I need to tell you something else about the night Randy went missing..."

He stared at her. "And what's that?"

The boy wandered in the room. "What are you guys talking about?"

"Nothing, sweetheart," Nancy said.

"That's okay... Daddy told me the truth... he said it was all about the finesse," he said.

"What did you say to him, Ron?"

"I didn't say anything."

"No... not Ron. My real daddy. I ran into him in the billiards room. I guess that's where I get my red hair. He said he used to live here, too."

The boy smiled, walking out of the room, his whistle echoing through the halls.

THE END

ABOUT THE AUTHOR

Writing term papers and essays in college and graduate school was only the genesis of Dan McDowell's career in wordsmithing. After eleven-years working in technology and business management, Dan's growing appetite for writing thrilling and chilling stories to escape the left-brained confines of Corporate America leaves him diving headfirst into the right-brained universe of fiction. He and his family currently reside in a restored 1903 home near San Antonio, TX.

NOTE FROM THE AUTHOR

Word-of-mouth is crucial for any author to succeed. If you enjoyed *Oak Hollow*, please leave a review online—anywhere you are able. Even if it's just a sentence or two. It would make all the difference and would be very much appreciated.

Thanks!
Dan McDowell

For fans of Dan McDowell, please check out our recommended title for your next great read!

Level Zero